Whisper Lane

With Love and Best Wishes

Elizabeth Walton

x xx.

Elizabeth Walton

authorHOUSE®

AuthorHouse™ UK
1663 Liberty Drive
Bloomington, IN 47403 USA
www.authorhouse.co.uk
Phone: 0800.197.4150

Published by AuthorHouse 07/25/2016

ISBN: 978-1-5246-3797-2 (sc)
ISBN: 978-1-5246-3798-9 (e)

Print information available on the last page.

Any people depicted in stock imagery provided by Thinkstock are models, and such images are being used for illustrative purposes only. Certain stock imagery © Thinkstock.

This book is printed on acid-free paper.

CONTENTS

CHAPTER ONE

James and Sally were out walking in the countryside. It was a beautiful day in early summer. It was pleasantly warm and a lovely day to be outside in the fresh air. James and Sally had driven out to a small village about ten miles from their home so that they could enjoy this lovely day, just the two of them, in the way they both really liked. This particular village, was very attractive, and a favourite of theirs. It was situated in open countryside so there were plenty of lovely walks around.

The vague plan, James and Sally had both made for the day, was to have a longish walk in the surrounding countryside and then to call in at the village pub for a drink and probably also a bite to eat.

James and Sally had known each other for just over two years and had sealed this relationship three months previously when they had got married. Both James and Sally had worked hard throughout this past week, busy with their respective jobs Monday to Friday, and then of course there were the routine household jobs the day before. Now it felt good on this pleasant Sunday to be out walking together and discussing their plans for their future. James and Sally had visited this small village of Marton cum Tiddleworth a few times in the past, but did not know the surrounding area very well, considering that it was only a short distance, just a few miles from where they lived.

The village was not very big but it was certainly very picturesque. They had left their car in the small village car park and had walked about five or six miles in a circle around the village, enjoying the very attractive scenery.

As they were coming to the end of their walk and were returning to the village, they noticed what appeared to be a rather tumbled down, old cottage. The cottage had a make shift sort of fence surrounding it, presumably it had been clumsily constructed in order to keep any intruders out. The cottage did have rather a neglected feel about it, as if it had been uninhabited for some time.

James and Sally lived in a small flat and had been looking for some time now for a more suitable home for their future together. The flat had initially been rented by James when he was still single. It had been the more obvious option, for Sally to move into James flat. Now though this flat was just too small for the two of them, there was certainly no way that they could ever contemplate increasing their family further while they were still living there.

They had both got into the habit, where ever they went and whenever they had the time, of looking at any prospective property that could possibly be a potential new home for them.

Together, while they were here, they both felt compelled to look across the fence at this cottage, they stood looking for several minutes, but both dismissed this cottage as being totally unsuitable. This old cottage did look somewhat neglected and would surely need too much work renovating it, before it could at least be habitable. This was certainly not the type of property that they had planned on purchasing. They both had visions of moving to a fairly new house on a new modern estate where there would be plenty of other young families.

Not only was this run down cottage not suitable for them, there was certainly no "for sale" sign anywhere to be seen on this property. James and Sally carried on with their walk. They finished the walk, as they had planned to do so, by calling in for a drink and a bit of lunch at the village pub.

This village of Marton cum Tiddleworth was very small, but it did have a decent pub. The pub was situated in the heart of the village. In front of the pub was quite a large village green, where there was also a duck pond. The pond was only quite small, but there were a few ducks floating on the surface.

The pub had the unusual name of The Duck and Cow. James commented on the name, one that he had never heard of before, but that somehow, for this pub it did kind of seem right. The name Duck and Cow had presumably been taken from the duck pond and the surrounding farm land, they had certainly seen plenty of cows whilst they were out walking. The village pub was very old and looked as if it had been there forever. This could be said for all of the houses in the village, there did not appear to be any new houses at all here.

James and Sally discussed over lunch how pleasant it would be to live in a village similar to this one, however they had not seen any houses at all that were for sale in this village, and they could not imagine that there would ever be any new houses built here. The thought of a new housing estate here would surely spoil the feel of the village.

Several weeks went past following their walk around the village of Marton cum Tiddleworth. James and Sally continued with their busy lives, both of them working quite hard throughout the week. James was an accountant and Sally a junior school teacher. Sally in particular, very frequently, brought home school work that had to be marked and also had to bring home lessons to be planned and so Sally was kept busy most evenings.

Sally did though like to try to keep the weekends free. They liked to spend the weekends together, and when they were able to do so, a lot of this spare time was spent house hunting. It was not easy though, none of the houses that they were looking at appeared to be really suitable. They were both looking for that special something, though at present neither of them seemed to know what that special something was. Most of the house hunting that they did was mainly on fairly new or very new housing estates. Many of these houses were suitable, and were on the type of housing estate that both of them had presumed they would eventually settle, but James and Sally dismissed many of them because they simply lacked character, or they were not affordable.

They had to carefully consider the location of their future home, it was very important that they were both able to get to work easily, neither of them liked the idea of having a lengthy commute to work, and neither of them wanted to change their jobs. James and Sally both though had the feeling that the right house would eventually turn up, and of course both hoped that when it did turn up then it would be that special something. They both hoped maybe eventually, they would look at a house and would know that this was the one.

One of the houses they went to look at was on a Saturday morning, and this also once again turned out to be rather disappointing. There was nothing really wrong with this house, the price was within their agreed budget, and the location was suitable, but the house just somehow seemed to be on the dull side and lacked character. This house, the one that they had looked at, was situated just a couple of miles outside the village of Marton cum Tiddleworth, in a neighbouring village.

Since they were in the area they decided to go and have lunch at the Duck and Cow pub again. They talked over lunch about the number of houses that they had already looked at and had not found suitable. "Do you think that we are setting our goals too high" suggested Sally. "We seem to be looking for the perfect house, one that we may never find." James had to agree. With the cost of their recent wedding and honeymoon they both knew they could not afford to increase the proposed budget that they had decided on for the house. "Perhaps," said James with a bit of a sigh, "we will have to set our sights a little bit lower, maybe we should consider one of these new builds, and just make a sacrifice on character or location, or maybe we should look at a few more older properties."

By the time they had finished eating the weather had improved. It had been drizzling for much of the morning but there was now a watery sun trying to get out. It was still on the cool side for summer but they had brought coats with them. They did not have any definite plans for the afternoon, apart from a bit of food shopping which could certainly wait until later, so they decided to stretch their legs and go for a gentle stroll. Their walk just automatically, without any discussion between them, took them on the same track that it had done a few weeks previously, which after a few miles around the village led them once again to the tumbledown cottage.

It had not changed at all, no one seemed to have been there, and it certainly had an abandoned air about it. They had already previously dismissed this house as being totally unsuitable, but for no apparent reason they spent quite some time just staring into it. They could not get too close to the cottage because of the fence but somehow they both felt drawn towards it, though they could not understand why.

James pointed out that it was completely impractical for them even to consider. There was not even a proper road leading down to it. The cottage was situated about one hundred yards down a dirt track, although despite this, it was still convenient for the village and in particular the village pub, which was only about a quarter of a mile away, it did somehow seem appealing, the thought of having the Duck and Cow as their local pub. It seemed silly though to base what could be their future home in an area where the biggest attraction was the cosiness of the village pub. Although the track was certainly no more than a bridle path it did have a name, Whisper Lane, as if maybe at one time it had been more of a proper road.

Neither of them had ever considered buying a house that needed so much work doing to it, they had both presumed they would buy a house where they would just be able to move straight into. Neither James or Sally were very practical when it came to DIY. The other houses they had looked at had mostly been situated on relatively new housing estates, where no DIY would have been needed. They had also not considered buying a house in such a rural location, though there was no real reason for this. They both had a car and this village would be an easy commute for both of them.

While they were stood there, trying to convince each other the merits for this run down house, neither of them had noticed a man watching them. He had paused for a few moments at the top of the lane. The man was maybe in his mid thirties, quite an ordinary slim built man, but with long wavy hair which he had fastened back in a ponytail. The man did stop to watch James and Sally just for a little while before he wandered off.

Sally did point out to James some of the possibilities with this cottage. If they bought this and did it up then they would probably get a considerably larger house for their money than they could currently afford. The house was certainly bigger than any that they had so far looked at, but also the garden of this house was very big as well. None of the houses that they had looked at so far had a garden anywhere near as large as this one.

Sally was looking towards the future, she could just imagine one day, sometime in the not too distant future, when the house was no longer tumbledown and the garden would also by then be all cleared and tidy, with a couple of children playing in it. Sally had to be practical though and really knew that this house was not for them, they would just have to continue looking elsewhere.

Over the following few weeks both of them continued to feel curious and drawn to this mysterious house, though they could not say why. It seemed to keep cropping up in conversations whenever they talked about house hunting, in a way that none of the other houses they had looked at did. They both knew though it was just not practical, this particular house was not what they had intended, but they still found that they did keep talking about it.

To satisfy their curiosity they decided to do some research to see if they could discover just who the actual owner of the property was. They decided if they did find out that the cottage was definitely not up for sale than they would then be able to forget all about it and continue with their search for a more suitable property, either way it would put their minds and their curiosities to rest and they would be able to carry on with a more intensive house hunting.

Together they did some research over the ownership of the cottage, which of course, called upon another visit to the Duck and Cow pub. Here the landlord was able to provide some information about the cottage. They were able to discover that the cottage was last owned by an elderly couple. The cottage has been left empty for just over a year since the couple who had owned it had both unfortunately died. They had lived there for a long time. However over the last few years of their lives they had grown older and frailer and so had not been able to do any maintenance on the property. The cottage had become somewhat dilapidated. "A few of the locals did offer to help with some of the maintenance work and the gardening, but they were quite a stubborn, independent couple and they refused any offers of help," the pub landlord informed them.

Sally, from the limited information they had been given was able to track down the solicitor who was looking after the property. Sally phoned the solicitor and she discovered unfortunately that the house was not actually up for sale. Now though that they had received this piece of news Sally found she was quite saddened. They had of course presumed this would be the case, since there obviously was no for sale sign, but Sally in particular was surprised at just how disappointed she was.

The reason the cottage was not up for sale at present was because the solicitor had not as yet been able to track down any next of kin for the previous owners. James and Sally did manage to visit the solicitor and they informed him that if by any chance the property did come up for sale than they could be interested in buying it. The solicitor was quite firm that he was not in a position to sell the house, but when he saw that the young couple both had a keen interest in the property he did give them permission to go and have a look at the house. The solicitor was aware that one of these days a decision would have to be made on the cottage and it would certainly be useful if there was someone who was actually interested in buying it. The cottage needed to be bought soon before it fell into very serious disrepair.

The following weekend both James and Sally set off together to look at the cottage. They now had in their possession the key to the large padlock on the fence and also of course the key to the cottage itself. Sally did not know why, but she felt somehow more excited about this viewing than she had been about any of the other properties they had seen so far. There was no logical explanation for this, except this house was very different to any of the others. Sally felt that she did not want to appear to be too excited just in case this was once again not going to be the house for them.

After a bit of a struggle with the locks, the one on the gate and the one on the door, both of which seem to have rusted up a bit, they did eventually manage to get inside the cottage. The solicitor had insisted that they should be very cautious when looking around as he was not sure just how safe, or not, the property was. James and Sally both entered the cottage rather nervously. The house was very dark and felt cold, which was not really surprising, considering it had been empty for possibly some time, maybe a year or so. There were cobwebs everywhere, it was virtually impossible not to walk through them. It was a lovely bright sunny day outside, although still a bit cold. Inside the cottage though the windows were in need of a good clean and did not, for this reason, let in much light. It did make all the rooms feel somewhat dingy. Fortunately they had thought to bring a torch each with them.

They entered the house into a large hallway with the stairs just in front of them. Even though it did all look somewhat grubby, this entrance hall was very impressive. To the left of them, as they entered into the hall, the first door led to what was presumably the sitting room. This sitting room was large with a big bay window. At the back of the sitting room and leading from it, was the kitchen. The kitchen was very outdated, it would need all new units fitting. The kitchen though turned out to be also a good sized room and it did include a rather useful walk in pantry. On the ground floor they found there was also a dining room situated at the back of the house, this led off from the kitchen There was also another decent sized reception room on this ground floor. Together they spent some time discussing the use of this room. They decided that this extra reception room would make a useful office for them both or, perhaps in the future a playroom.

Both Sally and James became aware of the way they were discussing the use of these rooms, it did seem to indicate they both very keen to own this house. Neither of them could remember previously, in any of the other houses that they had viewed, that they had such discussions about the use of space. "We really must remember," stated James practically, "that we may never be able to own this house." "I know," replied Sally, "but still it is great just to dream."

After spending some time having a good look and poke around at the ground floor, James and Sally very slowly and carefully climbed up the stairs. They were both pleasantly surprised to find that the stairs did actually appear to be sound, and also seemed to be safer than they had at first presumed. The upstairs of the house, just like the downstairs, did not reveal any unpleasant surprises. It all badly needed a good clean and redecorating, but all of the walls seemed solid enough. They were both pleased to discover that there were in fact five bedrooms up here, although the smallest of these was not much more than just a box room. As they both expected, the bathroom was very old fashioned, quite shabby, and very much in need of replacing. On the whole though, to James and Sally's amazement, the house did seem to be in less need of attention than they had at first expected, though neither of them could claim to be building experts.

Once they had finished exploring the house they spent some more time wandering around the garden. They had spent longer in the house than they had intended, once outside though they both realised again just how cold the house was. They both stepped outside, shivering, into the garden.

"The house would certainly feel a lot warmer if the windows were clean and would therefore be able to let in some natural light. Even so if we were able to buy this house we would also have to put in a good central heating system." Sally was certainly able to imagine warm and airy rooms with their own furniture in it. She could even picture the rooms, once they were newly decorated in a lighter colour, just how large and spacious all of this house could be.

The garden was even larger than they had at first thought. There was much more to the garden at the back of the house than they had originally been able to see. The garden of course was very much over grown and needed a lot of attention, but they could both see the potential the garden could bring. "Neither of us are gardeners, would we be able to manage all of this?" James asked of Sally. "Mmm, quite a large lawn to cut, but I am sure we will be able to cope with it. My mum is a keen gardener, if we were able to buy this property, I am sure that sure would love to come and give a hand. Mum has said a few times that she would like to have more space in her own garden for a larger vegetable plot, perhaps she could have that vegetable plot here."

Eventually and somewhat reluctantly James and Sally left the property ensuring that the locks were securely fastened. Once again neither of them had noticed that they were being watched from a distance by a man with long wavy hair.

On the drive back home they both had to admit they were very taken with the property. It was certainly not the kind of house that previously they had even considered buying. All of the houses that they had looked at so far were very different to this one. All of the previous properties that they had looked at had all been relatively new, and none of them would have needed much work before they could move in. All of the other houses they had previously looked at, they had both dismissed very quickly, but not this one, they spent a lot of time talking about this house.

Now though they had been able to have a good look at this house, they were both certainly very interested in buying it. It was very hard and so frustrating to actually make a decision on purchasing this house when in actual fact it was not yet up for sale. They both knew that if the circumstances were different, than they would certainly have been very tempted to put in an offer in for the house as soon as possible. That they had now been to have a look at the house, they knew they were setting themselves up for a big disappointment if they were to find that the house was never going to be sold, or that the price of it turned out to be way above their budget. They also both realised that whatever the cost was to buy the house in the first place, then they would also need a good bit of money left, in order to do all of the renovation work.

Sally though did have one suggestion. They were unable to return the key to the solicitor until after the weekend so Sally suggested that they have a word with her Dad to see if he would be able to have a look at the house with them the following day. If the house one day did come up for sale then Sally's Dad may have more of an idea about how much it was worth. Since Sally's Dad was a builder, this did seem a very sensible suggestion. Sally's parents lived not too far away, and were only too happy, and also somewhat curious to have a look at this cottage that James and Sally were now very keen on.

The four of them returned to the house the following day and Sally's Dad was quite impressed with the house. "I must have driven just a hundred yards or so past this house many times before, but I had no idea it was here." He agreed with James that the house did appear to be quite sound and most of the work needed, to make it habitable, would just be more or less cosmetic. The whole of the house obviously needed redecorating, and of course it needed a new kitchen and bathroom. Sally's dad suggested also putting in a small downstairs cloakroom, there was certainly space for this and it would be useful in the future. He was also able to suggest a way to make the pantry larger, without too much trouble, so it could also be used as a utility room as well as a pantry.

"The small box room could also be converted into a dressing room or an en suite for the master bedroom."

By the time the four of them had finished looking around they were all convinced that this was the house for James and Sally, they all had to agree it did indeed have great potential. The only one big remaining problem of course was that the house was not up for sale and furthermore they also had no idea what the asking price would be.

Sally managed to finish work on time for once on the Monday, so she was able to return the key to the solicitor. She usually stayed behind in school for some time after all the children had left for the day, to catch up on marking or for a staff meeting, but today she made sure that she left promptly.

The solicitor was somewhat curious as to what James and Sally had thought of the house. Sally informed the kindly solicitor that if it had been at all possible then they would love to put an offer in straight away. "Amazingly" replied the solicitor, "that just might be possible. Shortly after you collected the key the other day we received a letter from another solicitor up in Scotland. It appears that the previous occupants of the cottage had died intestate, but we very have recently discovered that the lady did in fact have a cousin in Scotland. This cousin is also quite elderly and is now living in a nursing home.

There is no chance, of course, that the cousin will ever want to live in the house and although she does have some family of her own, there are no relatives who have the time or inclination to travel down from Scotland to view the house. I do believe that all she wishes to do is to sell the house as quickly as possible. Although she is living in a nursing home, she is of sound mind so that she is able to make a decision about the property." "Have you any idea," asked Sally, "what these people would be asking for the price of the house?" The solicitor could not answer this question but did suggest that perhaps James and Sally themselves could put in a reasonable suggestion. "The family are planning to ask a local estate agent to do a valuation on the house."

Sally was quite taken aback by the good news, she could not wait to get home to discuss this surprising turn of events with James. They both spent some time talking about the house, which now they both had a really strong feeling they were destined to one day own. They had to keep reminding each other that it might not happen, they knew they could not afford to get too excited just yet. They spent most of the evening discussing the house and trying to decide the value of the property. Sally of course phoned her dad and told him about the turn of events.

James and Sally did spend some time over the following few days discussing a reasonable offer they could make on the property. They did not want to suggest a price that was too low so it would not be accepted, but they did also want to make sure, if they were fortunate enough to buy this property, that they would have enough money left over for all the renovation work. Sally, of course, conferred with her Dad and he was more than helpful, with his knowledge from working in the building trade. Between the three of them they did come up with a price which was within James and Sally's budget, and would also leave some money left over in the pot for all of the renovations that would be needed.

They informed the solicitor of their offer, the solicitor then had to put this in writing to the legal owners of the property. James and Sally had to wait patiently for a week or two, but then they were both pleasantly surprised to hear that the offer they had made had been accepted. The present owner of the house was very keen to sell it quickly, without too much hassle.

Once the price of the property had been agreed then the sale of the property went through surprisingly quickly. Sally, in particular, had so expected their offer to be turned down. They were both left wondering if perhaps they should have put in a lower offer, but at least now though the house was just about theirs and they still had some money left over for the much needed renovations.

After the price had been accepted, than the purchase of the property was made even faster than usual since there was no chain at all involved. James and Sally were renting their apartment and therefore they did not have a property to sell.

It was only a few short weeks later, after putting in the offer, that the house became theirs. The rightful owner of the house had only recently become aware that she did actually own this property, and was quite happy to accept the reasonable offer that James and Sally had made without any negotiation. Fortunately all parties concerned seemed to want the house to be sold as quickly as possible.

CHAPTER TWO

Once James and Sally had become the proud new owners of the run down cottage than they spent as much spare time as they could at the property. They did as much of the restoration work they could manage by themselves, with some help of course from friends and family, particularly Sally's dad, who was a great help.

James and Sally did not always have the opportunity to be there each evening. They soon realised that by the time they had both got home from work, and then had something to eat, it was usually too late to then drive the ten miles to the cottage. The evenings by now were also dark and getting colder. It was not too easy to get much done in the house in these conditions, there was no heating yet in the house and so it was very cold. They were there though just about every spare minute of the weekend.

Fortunately there was not too much structural work to be done, but the cottage did need a new kitchen and bathroom at the very least, before James and Sally were able to move in. There were also many other jobs to do, such as the decorating of the rooms they would be using straight away. The four spare bedrooms could wait until after they had moved in, there was no rush to decorate these.

Luckily the weather remained warm during the day, even though it was now into autumn. While the weather stayed this dry and mild James spent as much time as he could working on the outside of the house before the winter weather changed and it did become too cold and too wet. The most important jobs that needed doing to the outside were some essential pointing and also some minor repairs to the roof. The roof, quite fortunately, on the whole was sound but there were one or two areas on it that did require some attention.

James was not naturally a practical person and had only previously tackled very minor DIY jobs, but with instruction from Sally's dad he did find that he was more capable than he had at first thought and he found himself keen to tackle a lot of the repair work. James found that he was surprised to find that he was enjoying this work, and was also taking quite a pride in doing most of the work himself. James had not really been looking forward to the practical side of restoring the house. He did find though that it did make a difference when it was his own house he was working on. There was also the economic factor to consider, while they were able to do most of the jobs between them, than this did of course help to keep the costs down.

As the weather continued to be this good, considering that it was now almost October, James was able to take a few days holiday from work and he spent this time working on the house by himself. Sally joined him each evening, coming straight from work and bringing a picnic meal for them both to share. This usually included a flask of warm soup, as of course the house was still quite cold. Sally's dad did help as much as he could but on this particular week he was too busy with his own work to help James.

On the Friday of this week off from work, James found himself once more working on the house by himself. James was very keen to tackle the repairs that were needed to be done to the roof and he knew that today would be the best day to be going up on the roof. James had seen the weather forecast and had noted that after today the weather was going to turn much colder and wetter.

James was usually very sensible and he knew that it was not really a very clever idea for him to be working up on the roof by himself. James knew he should not have been working on the roof by himself today, when there was no one else around at the property, however it did seem to be too good an opportunity to miss. He had no idea when the weather would be this good again to enable him to finish the necessary repairs to the roof. James wanted to ensure that the roof was completely weather proof before the cold and wet winter weather did take hold. There was certainly plenty of work to be done on the inside of the house that James knew he could tackle when the weather did turn colder and wet.

James collected all the tools that he needed for working on the roof and put them carefully into the pocket of his overalls. James climbed up the ladder, first ensuring that it was quite secure, and then set to work on the roof. James had to check some areas of the roof tiles to ensure they were all still intact and had not come loose. James had already spent some time previously doing this job. When James had been up on the roof before though, he had been accompanied by Sally's dad who had given him some sound instructions on safety as well as how to ensure that all the roof tiles were secure. Today James did work as carefully and meticulously as he could and was very pleased with the progress that he was making.

Work on the roof was progressing well and James had almost completed all of this piece work when he dropped his hammer, it just seemed to slip from his fingers. "Drat" exclaimed James, annoyed at anything that slowed down his work, especially when he was this close to finishing. Without thinking about what he was doing, James automatically looked down to see where the hammer had landed. This was James rather big mistake. As he looked down, the ladder wobbled, James realised at this instant that the ladder was probably not as secure as he had thought it was, he really should have checked it more carefully.

James was about to climb down the ladder to retrieve his hammer and of course to ensure the stability of the ladder, when the ladder moved even more and James found himself suddenly falling. It all happened so suddenly that James was unable to reach out to grab hold of either the roof or gutter in order to stop his fall.

The fall must in reality have happened very quickly, just a second or two, but for James the time almost seemed to momentarily stand still. He could feel himself falling and was waiting for the impact as he landed on the stone floor beneath him. The impact did of course inevitably occur, but the landing was much softer, and happened more slowly and gently than James had expected. It was as if some kind of force had occurred that had slowed down and eased his fall.

James lay there for a few moments on the ground, he was unsure at first of just what had happened. When he had started to recover his senses James felt around his immediate surroundings. He was either unable to, or somewhat reluctant to move much more than just his right arm at first. James was amazed to find that he was actually lying down on straw. James did not know how this was possible when there was definitely no straw anywhere near his house, but very hard paving stones. James did wonder for a few moments if he had been knocked unconscious in the fall and that this was now some part of some strange dream.

Slowly though James did become more alert and more aware of both his body and of his surroundings. He did not appear to be in any pain, which was really quite surprising. As James looked around he could not believe just where he was. This certainly did appear to be his house but it looked somehow different. The house looked very much as if he had stepped back in time. This though was surely not possible. James sat up with a jolt trying to work out just where he was.

Not far from where he was sat James could see some chickens scrabbling about in the dirt. He certainly did not have chickens at his house. James was by now fully alert and was trying his best to take in the surroundings. Just next to the pile of straw that James was still sitting on he noticed a rather unusual flagstone, different from all the others. This particular one had a simple design on it. On just one corner of the flagstone, there was the shape of a star and a crescent moon. It was a strange thing for James to notice, considering his present circumstances, but this particular flagstone did seem to stand out from the others.

James slowly got up on to his feet. He did this very cautiously just to make sure that there were no broken bones or any other injuries, even though he had landed on straw rather than hard flagstones, James was still surprised to find that he did not appear to have any injuries at all. Although the straw was gentler then the hard surface outside of his house, it should still not have broken his fall in the way that it did.

Once James had stood up for a short while, he became reassured that there did not appear to be any serious harm done. James was not able to decide what to do next when he became aware that he could hear voices approaching. The voices were coming from around the side of the house. James found himself trembling. He was at present not really prepared to meet anyone. He did have this feeling that he was trespassing, though surely through no fault of his own. James felt that he must be trespassing, although was not this his own house? He could not think of any logical reason to explain to anyone as to why he was there. James had a sudden compulsion to move and put some distance between himself and the owners of the voices, he knew that he would not be able to give a reasonable explanation as to why he was there, and at present his mind was certainly not working logically. Before James did encounter anyone else he did want to try and find out just where he actually was.

James walked as quickly as he could in the opposite direction, away from the voices around the other side of the house. As he moved around the house James saw, just a few yards from him there was a barn. This house where James now found himself, was to all intent and purpose his own house, but different, and the house that James now knew so well certainly did not have a barn. James did not really have the time to consider this right now, he just wanted to escape from the owners of the voices. James moved quickly across the open space and towards the direction of the barn. Fortunately there was a small door at the side of the barn that had been left open. James entered the barn and stood away from the door, waiting to hear the sound of the voices but they seemed to have receded somewhere into the distance.

James then, while trying to calm his nerves, had a look around and took in some of the contents of the barn. The barn was quite cluttered and contained a wide range of very old fashioned looking farm equipment. The contents of the barn added to James fear that wherever he was right now than it certainly did not appear to be the twenty first century as it had been, just before he slipped off the roof. James was beginning to wonder if in fact he had fallen into a working farm museum but he knew that was just not possible.

The voices that James had been trying to escape from now seemed once again to be coming in his direction. He could hear voices approaching and they now suddenly seemed to be very close. James quickly moved to the back of the barn and hid himself behind some of the old farm machinery. James sank to his knees, partly through fear of being discovered, and also due to a sudden weariness that came over him. This weariness could have been caused by the shock of his situation, or from the fall itself. Fortunately the two men had only come into the barn to collect something that was situated just inside the door, and they did not stay around long enough to notice James.

Once he was sure that they had left the barn, James looked up from his hiding place and looked over to the barn door. He could see that outside there was a washing line full of clothes blowing in the gentle breeze. The washing, like the farm machinery seemed to come from another period in time. James had never before seen a washing line full of nappies, the only ones that he had ever come across were the disposable ones bought in a supermarket.

The weather did appear to be quite a pleasant day for late September, if this indeed was still September. There were just a few fluffy white clouds in the blue sky, although it was not that warm. James could not help notice that he seemed to have brought the good weather with him, this was one thing that had remained the same, although for all intent and purpose it was the same house.

James was now trying to recover from his shock and spent a short while slumped down on the floor just looking at the farm equipment without really seeing it. James was hiding down behind an old fashioned plough. James wanted to keep out of sight just in case the owner of this property decided to return again, and also from a general inertia. James was still frightened of being found by these farmers, he had no idea how he could explain to them his being there.

As James was taking in the sights in this barn he was now wondering how on earth he was going to return to his own house. He was also beginning to wonder if he had suffered from concussion during the fall and that perhaps he really did belong here in this period of time rather than 2004, maybe his life in the year 2004 was just a big dream or perhaps this was all one big nightmare. James decided that whatever was happening to him that he now really had lost the plot. Everything that he had seen from this farmhouse did seem to date back very roughly about one hundred years.

James sat for a while on the cold stone floor trying to decide just what to do. As James had been sitting there for several minutes, or maybe much longer, he became aware of a sound. James looked up and there standing only a few feet away was another man. There was no getting away from this man as he was stood looking directly at James. He must have walked into the barn very quietly. This man though did not look as threatening and scary as the other two had done. James instinctively felt that this was someone in whom he could trust.

This man was of a fairly slim build and appeared to be slightly older than James. His hair was quite long, just past shoulder length, it was wavy and with a lot of grey in it. James was rather taken aback by what the man was wearing. He only appeared to be wearing a rather strange pair of trousers, they were somewhat baggy but fit close in to his ankles. On his feet he had on a pair of sandals. James thought that it was rather odd that he was bare above the waist, he must surely be very cold, but then many strange things had occurred in this short space of time and this could still be part of a dream.

"Hello" said James. "Please could you tell me where I am? I seem to be a bit lost, I am not even sure just how I arrived here." The stranger smiled down at James and knelt down next to him. "Hello, my name is Antonio. I am not sure how you came to arrive at Buttershaw farm, but this is where you are right now." "Please," asked James, "could you tell me what the date is?"

"Certainly, it is 24th September 1904." James was stunned, he had realised that everything around him did appear to be different, but how could he have possibly travelled back one hundred years. More important though was how on earth was he was going to get home again? He looked up imploringly at this stranger as if he could possibly have the answer. Antonio was no longer smiling but still had a kindly look on his face. "Would you like a lift back home?" he asked. James had had so many surprises in such a short period of time, but he was still stunned with this reply. It was as if Antonio knew just where he lived and all about the small problem of time travel, James was more than certain by now that he had indeed travelled back in time.

The surprises of the day though were not yet over. While they were talking Antonio had been facing towards James and so James had not seen his back. Now James heard a strange noise, a sort of rustling, creaking noise. Antonio's chest seemed to expand while James was looking at it, and then a large pair of wings appeared from his back. This felt a little bit like a scene from The Incredible Hulk, but what was happening to Antonio was much more graceful and gentle.

Before James had a chance to say anything he found himself being swept up off the floor where he had still been kneeling, and into one of these wings. It felt strong and secure but also soft and warm. It was amazing that this large secure pair of wings had appeared from just one rather slim man. James had no choice but to curl up in this pair of wings as it cocooned him. Although Antonio had not appeared to be that large, there did now seem to be plenty of space here on his back between the wings for James to curl up in.

Once James was safe and secure on his back, Antonio walked the few steps out of the barn and with a large, but graceful leap he took off into the air. Instinctively and with some help from Antonio, James shifted his weight on Antonio's back so that Antonio had better use of his wings. James felt them both soaring up towards the sky. This should be so scary and very, very strange but James thought that it actually felt quite exhilarating. It certainly took his mind off the fall, the time travel and the near encounter with the menacing looking farmers.

They did not seem to have been flying for very long when James realised that they were now descending. While James was there on Antonio's back he was so amazed by the whole concept of the journey that he was not able to consider the actual scenery or where they were travelling to at all. Antonio could have been taking him anywhere. This was all so surreal but at the same time so thrilling. James was barely able to see over Antonio's shoulder, he had no idea at all where they were going. Antonio could be taking him safely home, or he could be taking him to the end of the earth, at present though James just felt quite safe.

The next thing that James knew was that he was waking up, although he had not realised that he had indeed fallen asleep. He was lying on the floor just next to his house. The hammer that had fallen from his grasp on the roof was now just there, only a few feet away, also the ladder was there laid out across the ground where it must have come crashing down. There was no sign at all of what must have been surely an angel, an angel with long wavy hair.

James was now laid there wondering if he really had fallen from the roof and had he suffered from concussion. He had obviously just had a very strange dream. James lay there trying to recall his dream. At the same time as he was trying to recall the events that had just happened to him, James was also mentally trying to work out, once again, if any part of him hurt, and if he was suffering from any injuries. He did not appear to be in any pain at all though.

As James was laying there thinking that he should be getting up, he heard the noise of a car trailing down the dirt track towards the cottage. He had, not surprisingly, quite lost track of time and was now amazed to realise that Sally had finished work and here she was arriving home. The next thing he knew was Sally bouncing around the corner. She stopped abruptly when she saw James just lying there. "I thought that you would be working hard, what on earth are you doing lying on the ground?" said Sally.

James looked rather sheepish and slowly he did get up. He certainly could not feel any injuries. Although it had been a pleasant sunny day, it was now late September, and it was fairly cold. Even though there did not appear to be any injuries, James was now certainly beginning to feel really cold. "You will not believe what has happened to me today" said James. "Try me" answered Sally who actually now was a bit concerned and somewhat puzzled that James had been lying there on the cold hard floor. James was by now starting to shiver with the cold.

Together they wandered inside and made a cup of tea before James told Sally his story. He told her about the fall from the roof and then about his apparent strange dream. Sally was quite amazed by the tale and also concerned that James had not hurt himself. "You do need to be extra careful when you are working up there alone, could it not have waited until tomorrow." James explained about the weather forecast and how he wanted to hurry and finish this job. James was very impatient to get as much work on the house done as was possible, before the winter really did set in.

They sat together for some time discussing the encounter with the angel, if he really was an angel, and the journey back one hundred years. They both decided that it must have been a dream and maybe a touch of concussion. There was no other possible explanation for it. "I am just so amazed," said Sally, "that you have not injured yourself, not even a scratch or bruise, you were very lucky. Even if this was all just a strange dream you certainly must have fallen off the roof. Why on earth have you not got any injuries at all?"

"It did feel so real though" said James quietly. "Anyway no rest for the wicked, let's get back to work." Even though James should have been quite shaken up by his adventure he suddenly felt keen and full of energy, ready to continue with some task on the house and stood up ready to go back outside. "I would prefer if you would keep off the roof" said Sally, "at least for today, just in case you really did have a bump on the head and now have concussion, after all, my dad will be here tomorrow to help. It will be easier and a lot safer with the two of you working up there." "That is fine" replied James. "There are plenty more jobs that I can be getting on with for the rest of today."

Despite the strange experience that James had just had, he did not feel at all tired any more, but quite energetic and happy to continue with the work on the house, although he was also very keen to keep off the roof for the rest of the day.

CHAPTER THREE

The following day James was working on the house once again, but this time though he had some help from Bob, Sally's dad. Neither James nor Sally wanted to tell her dad about the accident since there was obviously no harm done and they did not want to worry him, or have to go through a lecture on health and safety! James just did not want to confess that he had been working up on the roof when there had not been anyone else around, it really was quite a stupid thing to have done. James also guessed that Sally did not really believe his story, he was sure that Bob would definitely not believe it.

The weather forecast proved to be accurate and the weather was no longer as good as it had been. Neither of the men felt like working on the roof since it was drizzling quite heavily and would have been dangerous up there. They decided instead to have a look in the cellar. They wanted to see how sound the walls of the cellar were and to make sure that there were no signs of any damp.

There was also quite a lot of junk down there in the cellar that had been left by the previous owners. They had the use of a skip at present, but only for a few more days, so James and Sally's Dad decided to spend some time clearing out the junk to see if any of it was actually worth saving and also to see the potential in the cellar. James and Sally wanted to have some idea if the cellar could perhaps be used for another room in the future, other than just a place to store unwanted junk, it was hard to decide at present just what to do with it when it was so full of the previous owner's possessions.

James, Sally and her dad, Bob spent an hour or so carrying unwanted rubbish upstairs and out into the skip, most of the junk was not worth saving. "It does seem rather sad," commented Sally "that we are throwing away all of this, that at one time could possibly have been someone's precious possessions." Sally was rather distracted at times with the job in hand when she kept finding some interesting piece of junk. They could not keep it all though and she knew that she had to be quite ruthless and throw most of it away.

While they working there down in the cellar, James noticed in one corner a flagstone that had previously been covered by some of the junk. The whole floor was dusty and dirty, it was a bit difficult to make out individual flagstones. The entire cellar floor was covered in flagstones, but this particular one caught James eye, he had seen one just like it only the day before. This flagstone also had on it a star shape and another shape, that of a crescent moon.

Bob noticed that something had caught James attention and he went over to have a look. Bob also commented on the flagstone, that it was quite unusual. "I have been a builder for a long time, but I have never seen a flagstone like that one before." James did not like to tell his father in law that he had seen another flagstone with the same design on just the previous day, but also agreed with him that it was somewhat unusual.

Two or three hours later they decided to stop for the day. The weather had not improved at all but they had now cleared up most of the rubbish from the cellar. The majority of this rubbish had to go into the skip, very little of it was worth salvaging.

The cellar did seem to be quite sound and dry, and did now appear to be considerably larger than they had first thought, now that it was clear from all of the rubbish that must have accumulated over the years. Once they decided to stop work for the day Bob, once he had got cleaned off as best as he could, went home for his tea which he knew his wife, Ruth, would have waiting for him.

James and Sally also decided to tidy themselves up, they both felt very grubby. Once they were reasonably clean they went to visit the local pub so that they could have something to eat there. They had visited the pub two or three times previously, but never before in the evening and they had not actually been in there for a few weeks, not since they had taken over the ownership of this cottage. There never have seemed to have been the time over the last few weeks.

Although there was still a lot of work that had to be done in the house, before it would become anything like comfortable, James and Sally did now like to sleep there at least one night a week. This is what they had planned to do on this particular night. The accommodation in their house was naturally very basic at present. They still had to move most of their furniture in and so for the time being they had to sleep on a mattress on the floor. Staying at the cottage though did make it feel more as if it was their own home. Although they really did now own this house, they both knew that it would not feel truly theirs until they had fully moved in. It was also of course more practical for them to be staying there. When they did stay at the cottage they did not have to spend so much time travelling and it gave them more time to spend on all of the renovation work that was needed to make it really habitable.

On the walk to the pub James mentioned again the unusual flagstone that they had uncovered down in the cellar. James had not been able to say anything about it in front of Sally's dad but now he was able to tell Sally that he had seen this flagstone before. "It was in the dream that I had yesterday after I slipped off the roof."

James still knew that it must have just been a dream, but somehow it all seemed too real and now it was just too much of a coincidence seeing this same strange flagstone. James was certain that he could not have seen the flagstone in their house before, since this was the first time that they had moved all the rubbish and uncovered the flagstone. He was sure that he had never before seen another flagstone quite like it.

Their house was situated slightly off the beaten track down its own road, but it was still very close to the small picturesque village. There were very few amenities in the village. There was no school and only one small shop, but at least it did have the pub. The pub did seem to be the very heart of the village. Marton cum Tiddleworth was also situated just a few miles from the nearest town which had all the amenities that the two of them needed. The village was also slightly more convenient for both of them to get to work than where they were currently living. They both felt that life would be easier once they had moved out of their flat and were living in this cottage permanently and they could not wait for this day to happen.

When James and Sally arrived at the Duck and Cow they were served by the landlord. James introduced themselves to the landlord, they had never introduced themselves properly before on their previous visits, they had only felt like visitors to the village on those occasions. James explained that they had managed to buy the cottage, the one that they had previously inquired about in the Duck and Cow, and were now busy carrying out all necessary repairs so that they could move in.

James and Sally were pleased to discover that their new local pub had a varied menu and did serve some decent food in the evening. When they had both set off to the pub, neither of them had been that sure that the pub actually did serve food on an evening. They had had only a light snack and drink there previously on a lunch time, but not a full evening meal. Today they had only eaten a sandwich at lunchtime at home. That was several hours ago and they had been working hard all day. Now they were now both very hungry and looking forward to the food they had ordered.

While they were waiting for their food to arrive, they spent some time chatting to some of the locals. Several of their new neighbours were interested to hear about the renovations and were keen to hear about the progress of it all, especially since the cottage had been empty and neglected for some time. One or two of the neighbours made some vague offers of help, James was not really sure if these were genuine offers or not.

As James and Sally were talking to their new neighbours and friends they asked about the history of the village. They discovered that the village dated back to at least the middle of the 18th century. Most of the village in fact was actually dated from about this time, with very few houses having been built since then.

James and Sally were already aware that there were quite a few rather grand houses in the village, these included Marton cum Tiddleworth Manor and Marton cum Tiddleworth Hall. Most villages of this size would perhaps have one large manor house but Marton cum Tiddleworth did seem to have more than its fair share of rather grand houses. One or two of these larger houses had been, some time ago, converted into executive flats. There were of course quite a number of smaller more modest houses including a few rows of terraced houses, that at one time would have been used by farm labourers. There were also several farms, most of these, situated on the outskirts of the village. Both James and Sally got the impression that this was quite a close knit community. A community where everyone knew each other very well, but even though they were the outsiders, they were still made to feel more than welcome.

James and Sally spent two or three quite enjoyable hours in the pub, including an excellent meal, before they had to return to their rather basic accommodation. They did have sufficient facilities to at least make a warm drink, but certainly not enough to be able to cook a full meal. Several times Sally had brought along a picnic meal of bread, cheese, salad and fruit, and also a bottle of wine. This kind of meal though was not very warming now that winter had set in. Having a meal at the cottage had saved them some time, they did not have to finish working too early, but instead were able to carry on with the renovation until well into the evening.

Tonight though, as they walked back to their cottage, they decided quite easily that they would do the same again the following weekend, visit the pub again and have another bar meal there. "You never know" said Sally, "we may be able to dig a bit deeper into the local history and find out if anyone knows anything about the unusual flagstone." "That's a good idea," replied James. "It could possibly confirm if that experience I had yesterday, really was just a dream." Neither of them had thought to mention the flagstone this evening when they were sat in the pub.

When they had returned to their cottage they spent some time, over a hot drink, discussing all the work that still needed to be completed before they were able to move in properly. They had intended to carry out all the renovations themselves, with some help from friends and family. Now though it seemed to make common sense that they should employ someone on a short term basis to give a hand. At present they were still having to pay out the rent for their apartment, as well as also paying for the mortgage on the cottage. They knew the sooner they were able to move into this cottage completely, than they would be saving quite a lot of money by not having to pay for the rent.

They wanted to employ someone with a good reputation but had no idea just who. Sally's dad did have a lot of contacts in the building trade, but each and everyone one of these contacts always seemed to be busy. They decided to postpone this decision until the following weekend and then they could ask in the village pub to see if there was anyone local who may available to help.

The following week James was back at work. They managed to make that extra effort and they spent most evenings at the cottage by going straight from work. It did make the days quite long and hard but the effort was worthwhile. They did seem now to be making quite reasonable progress.

They had borrowed a small fridge and had taken their microwave out of the apartment so Sally could prepare a basic meal each evening. They were both surprised by how much they managed to achieve on the restoration work by being there on an evening. The following weekend they stayed for the full weekend as planned and then they went to the pub for a meal on the Saturday evening. They were warmly greeted again by the pub landlord and by some of the other locals they had met the week before.

While they were there at the pub they were able to gather some more information about their house and also about the village. They were given a lot of information about the couple who had lived in their cottage before them. James and Sally learned that the previous owners of their cottage were very popular in this small village. The couple apparently did not have any children and there was also very little mention of any other relatives, it became apparent that any family that they did have lived a long way off and never seemed to be able to come for a visit. This was presumably why the cottage had been empty for so long, while the solicitors had been trying to track down these little known relatives. Despite this lack of obvious family, the couple were always cheerful and kept themselves fit and active. They had remained busy well into old age and then died within a few weeks of each other. It was not mentioned how this couple had died and Sally decided that she really did not want to know, she did not like to think that perhaps they had died, possibly even in sad or mysterious circumstances, in their cottage.

After they had finished eating, James mentioned the unusual flagstone they had come across in the cellar, the one with the moon and star shape. Unfortunately though none of the locals they asked were able to provide any information on the flagstones. Several of them had visited the cottage previously but none of them had been down into the cellar so had therefore not seen this flagstone. James realised that of course even if they had been down into the cellar they would not necessarily seen the flagstone as it would probably have been covered up. James and Sally were a little disappointed that they were not able to shed more light on the mystery of the unusual flagstone, but still they passed on a pleasant few hours in the pub.

Before they left James asked the landlord if he knew by any chance, of anyone who would be able to help them with some of the restoration work on the cottage. The landlord, Dave, was able to come up with one suggestion. He mentioned a man called Tony who lived about a half a mile away on the edge of the village he was quite good at building work, and seemed to be able to turn his hand to a lot of DIY jobs. Dave told James that Tony had on several occasions helped out with some repairs and maintenance in the pub, as well as now and again helping out behind the bar. The pub landlord went on to say that Tony was both reliable and hard working. He was able to give James his phone number.

It was very dark when James and Sally eventually left the pub and walked home together, hand in hand, back to their cottage. It was very cold now, the weather had turned much more wintry. The sky tonight though was clear, hardly a cloud in sight. Sally looked up to enjoy the starry sky. There was very little light pollution out here in the countryside and it really did seem to make a difference to the night sky. As Sally gazed up she was lucky enough to see a shooting star. Sally cried out in surprise over this rare occurrence, but fortunately she also remembered to make a wish. It was one of those very special moments that reinforced their decision to move to this village and to their cottage. They both knew that they had done the right thing by buying this run down cottage.

The following day James rang Tony. The pub landlord had reassured James that Tony would not mind being disturbed on a Sunday and that he did have permission from Tony to pass on his phone number, if anyone needed any odd jobs doing. They arranged for Tony to call round that afternoon so that they could discuss the work that still needed to be completed on the cottage, and to find out which of these tasks Tony could help them with. A few hours later, as arranged, Tony knocked on the door. James went to let him in and knew that he had seen Tony before. At first James was not sure when or where they have met previously, but then he remembered, it was probably his long wavy hair, that was now fastened back in a pony tail, that gave it away. James realised the only time that he had met Tony before was during his strange dream, that this Tony, who was now stood before him, was also the angel Antonio.

For a few seconds James was at a loss as to what to say. He motioned for Tony to enter into the hallway then had to ask "Do I know you from somewhere?" Tony replied that he had lived in the village for a long time in fact all his life and that James had probably just seen him around, maybe at the pub. James knew that it had been more than just a chance encounter in the village or the pub, but he could not exactly ask if Tony was really an angel!

James had to put his shock and surprise to one side for a while. He found he was able to conceal his inner thoughts and discuss with Tony the plans they still had for the cottage. They were also able to come to some arrangements for when Tony would work. Tony seemed to be quite a general handy man around the village and did do a lot of work for several of the other villagers, he seemed to be able to turn his hand to a variety of tasks. James hoped that Tony would be as reliable and efficient as he appeared to be. Between them they arranged that Tony would work every Saturday with James on the cottage, and also on two other days during the week, when he would mostly have to be working by himself.

Over the next few weeks, with Tony's help, work on the cottage progressed at a much faster pace than they could have hoped for. They found Tony really was quite an asset and just wished they could have employed him sooner. During this time, with Tony's help and with other professional help, they were able to fit both the kitchen and the bathroom and also complete most of the decorating.

Tony soon became quite a godsend in that he was able to supervise other workmen while James and Sally were at work, as well as getting along with a lot of the jobs by himself.

Once most of this work was done, James and Sally moved out of their flat and went to live full time in their cottage. Tony was again very useful when it came to the moving in day, as he had his own van, and between the three of them and also with some help from Sally's parents and a few friends, they were able to move all the furniture and belongings, with only two trips required back and forth. The apartment that James had been renting for several years, had been on the small side, so they had not accumulated too much furniture. Now though with all of their furniture and soft furnishings installed in the cottage, it did still look very bare. They both knew they would slowly buy more furniture over a period of time, and also more soft furnishings would make the cottage feel more homely. For now though they had everything that they needed to live in the cottage quite comfortably.

That evening, to celebrate the big move, they went once again to the local pub. They had now become regulars there and they were always warmly greeted, tonight though seemed even more special. Tony was also at the pub on this evening so even though they had paid him a reasonable wage for all the work that he had done, they were also able to buy him a drink or two to say thank you. Now they had actually moved into the cottage they really felt as if they did belong

47

there in the village. It was also a weight off their minds now they were no longer having to pay for the rent on the apartment as well as the mortgage, not to mention the time they would save by living in only one place and the shorter journeys they both had in commuting back and forth to work.

CHAPTER FOUR

Throughout this time, since they had first bought the cottage, James and Sally had spent a lot of time on the house itself but very little time in the garden. The weekend after they moved in, with some help from her mum, Sally spent some time trying to restore some sort of order to the garden. It was now early December but the village was enjoying another dry spell. There had been a slight frost overnight, but by mid morning the sun was out and it felt almost warm. The day seemed too good to be spent indoors. Sally and her mum, Ruth, spent some time trying to decide which areas of the garden could be saved and which needed to be totally transformed. There was a lot of sorting out to be done but Sally began to realise, with help from her mum, who was quite a keen gardener, that with careful weeding and pruning then there were many beautiful plants in the garden that could be saved and brought back to life.

Running along the back of the cottage there was a big old wall which gave the cottage plenty of privacy. Sally and her mum on this Saturday made this area at the back of the cottage the starting point for the gardening. As they were working together in this shaded area they managed to clear much of the weeds and debris from the paved area. Quite a lot of the garden at the front and back surrounding the cottage was made up of the same flagstones. There was though a large lawn to the front of the property.

Sally gave an exclamation when she came across another unusual flagstone. It had the same design on it as the other one that they had uncovered in the cellar, that of a star and a crescent moon. They had not seen this particular flagstone before, as it had been well hidden under the weeds that had been growing across the path. James had been working on the front garden, now he stopped what he was doing and came round to have a look. It really was just the same as the other one that they had seen in the cellar, and the one that James had seen in his "dream", as both James and Sally thought of his strange occurrence. It was a mystery though as to why these flagstones should be there, Sally was now even more interested to know how long they had been there, if they were as old as the house, and where they came from. Sally was curious to know why this particular design, if it did have any meaning to it. For the time being though this would have to remain a mystery.

Discovering this other strange flagstone did give Sally some encouragement to carry on with the rather large task of clearing the garden, she was curious to know if there were any more of these rather strange flagstones. During the afternoon though they did only find the one out at the back, but they did continue to realise the potentials of this garden and just how beautiful it could eventually become.

Round at the side of the cottage was a very old outbuilding. It had probably been there as long as the house had. This outbuilding had a rather large old padlock on it. The padlock was very rusty. James had looked at the padlock soon after they took ownership of the cottage but decided at that time to leave it until sometime in the future when he would have more time. Now most of the work in the house had been completed James decided to have another look at this old outbuilding and see if he could now remove the lock. The building was not that big but was brick built and would probably be useful in the future for storing garden equipment.

They had never been given the key to this padlock, presumably it had been lost some time ago. James had been more than a bit curious about this building but he had not, up until now, had the time to have a proper look at it, and they had not yet been able to get inside it.

The day after Sally and Ruth had been working on the garden with a determined effort James managed to cut the old rusty padlock off and gained access to this somewhat dilapidated outbuilding. Inside he found a lot more junk, most of which had probably been there for donkeys years. There were many items that would have presumably originally have come from their cottage, old kitchen equipment that had been dumped here once it stopped working, and quite a lot of other old paraphernalia. All of these objects presumably the previous couple had apparently not liked to throw away. James came to the conclusion that this couple must have been hoarders because of the amount of junk that they had left behind in the cellar and now all of this in the outbuilding. This job of disposing of all this old property was now left for James and Sally to tackle.

James had now realised that clearing out all of this junk was turning out to be a fascinating task, all of this stuff must have quite a history behind it. James knew that they would certainly have to be careful that they did not throw away anything of value.

They did not need any more storage space at present, there was more than enough room in the cellar, not to mention the large attic, and a couple of empty bedrooms. They had still not had enough time yet to really investigate the attic, or to decide what to do with it. The attic could just be left as a storeroom, or it did also have great potential to be turned into another bedroom, though they did not really need another bedroom.

James could see that this old outbuilding would be very useful sometime in the future, if for nothing else than they could at least keep their gardening tools in it. They had already acquired a few basic gardening tools, most of which had been donated by Ruth. James knew though in the future because of the size of the garden they would be in need of plenty more tools, including a decent lawn mower, when the following summer came around.

James made his way to the back of the old brick shed, he sneezed a few times because of the dust he had disturbed. At the back of the outbuilding James was surprised to see what looked like an old door but this door was very solid looking and was actually made up of bricks. It was almost as if there had been a proper door there sometime previously, but for some reason it had been bricked up.

James studied this strange brick door for a few minutes trying to puzzle out why anyone would have made a door here of bricks. He could not decide if it was an actual door or if it had at one time been a door that someone for some reason had more recently bricked up.

It was a strange place to have a door in the first place as this outbuilding was just not large enough to need two doors. There must have been a door to the back of this outbuilding at one time, a door that probably led to the fields at the back. Whoever had created this unusual brick door since then, they seemed to be protecting the building from something. Surely though a good strong wooden door would have done, since there were only fields at the back. As James puzzled over the door he noticed in the bottom left hand corner something that had appeared to have been chiselled into the brick work. On closer inspection James could see that this was another crescent moon and star, very similar to, but smaller than the ones that he had seen on the flagstone.

James felt that he needed to get a better look at this strange door so he went back into the cottage and returned with a torch they kept handy. Sally was not at home, she was out doing a large supermarket shop while James was exploring this outbuilding. James knew that she would be gone for another hour or so yet. For the time being he was unable to share this news with her, if it was news, though it really probably wasn't anything significant. James was curious enough now to try to find out and see if the door did actually open. He knew that he really should be spending the time trying to clear out this building but he felt compelled to look at this door more closely first. He just knew that he wouldn't be able to get on with anything constructive until his curiosity had been satisfied.

If the door did actually open, then James had to presume that it would surely open out to the back of the property, and into the field beyond. James though still wanted to try, he did not know why this part of the old building was catching his attention so much, but he just felt compelled to investigate it further. After giving this solid brick door a few hefty shoves James was about to give up. Just before he did stop trying to open this strange door though, he bent down so that he could have a closer look at the star and moon shape. James put his hand on these shapes and instinctively gave them a push. James did not expect anything to happen, but the next thing he knew was that the door did open outwards. These shapes seemed to be the key to unlocking the door.

James walked through the door and found that he was standing at the back of the old outbuilding in what could have been at one time part of his garden, or more likely the field beyond. Once again this view was quite different to the view James was now more than familiar with. With dawning James realised he was back once again on the property of a certain farm house, the one that had been a part of his previous strange dream. James had previously walked all the way the around the garden of his cottage, and it had not looked like this. There were fields at the back of their cottage, but this scenery somehow looked different. There were still fields here, but the boundary of the fields had changed and although James was certainly no farmer, he did know that the crop in this field was different to the one that was growing in 2004.

James looked around, once again astounded. As James was stood there taking in the sights around him, he had not realised that the door that led back into his outbuilding had closed behind him, he was hardly aware that he had taken a step or two away from the door, and now the door had closed behind him. James though did suddenly realise that he was once more trapped in another period of time.

While James was so busy looking at these sights and trying to compare them with his own garden, he had not been aware someone was watching him. James turned round and saw who he thought was presumably the farmer, the one that owned this land in this present time. The farmer just seemed to think that James was one of the farm hands and asked him not too politely to return to work.

James felt he had no choice but to follow the direction in which the farmer was pointing. Once again he could not think of an explanation as to why he was trespassing on this farmers land. The farmer was pointing to a nearby field. There were already several farm labourers here in the field and before James could think of anything sensible to say he found himself helping out on the farm. James went obediently on to join the other workers and before he knew it he had spent what felt like two or three hours helping out on the farm. They were mainly cutting hay. The other farm workers did not pay too much attention to James, one or two of them just gave a nod of the head as James approached them.

James found that he had to very quickly learn how to use a scythe. This rather surprisingly, he managed to do so without giving himself away as an imposter and without causing injury to himself or anyone else. As well as being rather scared that he would be found out, James was also very curious to know more about this working farm, this farm which could possibly be one hundred years in the past. James at present could not come up with an excuse to leave his work and try to find a way back into his own world, but he was also so very curious about this strange world that he seemed to have now chanced upon.

James knew that the last time he had visited this farm, it was just one hundred years earlier than the life he knew. This could not be exactly one hundred years ago, not this time, they would surely not be cutting hay in December? The weather he had left behind had been mild for December but this weather here was too warm, it must be about September time James decided. James though was a bit clueless to farm life, and he was not really sure exactly when hay was cut. He did not like to ask this question of any of his fellow workers though, they would surely think he would be very strange not knowing the exact date, let alone which season of the year they were in.

After quite some time had passed, which had been spent in cutting hay the labourers stopped to eat lunch. James had just been beginning to think that he was too exhausted to carry on with the manual labour for much longer, so he was really glad of the rest. James was used to office work and was finding this manual work, certainly a change, but very exhausting.

The farm workers sat to eat lunch underneath the shade of an old oak tree. James had of course not got any lunch with him and made some vague excuse for not bringing any with him. Several of the men though were quite happy to share their lunch with James. James did find that he was surprisingly hungry after all the work and was very pleased to be tucking into a big chunky sandwich.

James kept fairly quiet while they were eating lunch so he did not give himself away. James was very easily able to understand the conversations that were going on around him but the dialect was quite different from his own. James was aware that if he did speak too much than he would raise some curiosity about his accent, he really did not want to be quizzed about where he came from, so mostly James sat in silence taking in the sights and sounds around him.

They were not able to sit for too long over lunch, James had only just recovered from the exhausting morning before he found he was back at work again, once more cutting hay. The time seemed to pass by quickly but all the time at the back of his mind, James was concerned about either being found out, or just how on earth he was going to return home. Sally must surely be home now and would be wondering where he was.

Just as James was thinking that he could no longer go on, partly because of sheer exhaustion, and also from fear of being found out, he did realise all of the workers were now moving on. They went to a water pump not far from the farm house. James began to then realise, from the talk around him, that the next job that they had to do was to milk the cows. James now became very worried as he had never milked a cow in his life before, learning how to use a scythe was one thing, but James was not happy at all about the prospect of milking cows.

Somehow when no one was looking James managed to slip away from his fellow farm labourers and was able to escape into the old barn where he had escaped to previously. When he got into the barn James slumped into the same corner he had used on the previous occasion when he had to hide. James was very tired but he was also hot. The weather on this farm had been different, warmer than the cold winter weather that he had left behind and to which James now longed to get back to.

James was sat there for some time wondering just what to do. He glanced down at his hands, he had thought that they felt a bit sore, but on closer inspection he found that he did have two or three blisters. James glanced up when he heard someone enter the barn. He thought that it might have been the farmer coming to look for him. Fortunately though it was a much friendlier, more welcome face, the angel Antonio had returned. Antonio greeted James kindly, but made no mention of the fact that he had been working with James helping to restore the cottage or that the two of them had even met before. "Would you like a lift home?" asked Antonio, "or would you like to stay and help out on the farm for a while longer?" "I would love a lift home" replied James, "that is if you happen to be going in my direction?"

Once again Antonio unfurled his wings and encouraged James to climb onto his back. This still seemed so unreal to James but with no other means of returning to his own world he climbed on to Antonio's back, which had now broadened and seemed to accommodate him very well. No sooner had James climbed on to Antonio's back than they were once more lifting up into the air and James was on his way home. While they were up in the air James just felt so warm and comfortable and after all the hard physical labour he found that he was unable to keep awake and found himself drifting off to sleep. Half awake and half asleep James did vaguely wonder if he was safe enough, it did cross his mind that he could quite easily fall off Antonio's back, but he felt so well supported and somehow confident that Antonio would deliver him safely home.

The next thing James was aware of, was waking up at the back of the old outbuilding in his back garden. It was not too comfortable laying there on the hard ground but James felt quite content, as if he were just waking up from a pleasant dream in his own bed. It was also though very cold on the solid floor but James felt quite warm on the inside, it must have been from all the hard work that he had done on the farm. When James woke up, Antonio was nowhere to be seen, James would have liked to have thanked him for coming to his rescue once again. It was also strange that just like previously James had seemed to have been asleep when Antonio did deliver him safely back into his own world. James wondered vaguely, as he was slowly waking, if anyone had seen an angel descending from the sky with him on his back.

James was just starting to stir himself when he heard Sally calling out. He had not heard her car as she came back from her shopping trip. James presumed that Sally must have been back for some time since he felt as if he must have been gone for several hours. Hearing Sally's voice James quickly roused himself from his dream like state and left the old outbuilding and went to see if she needed a hand with the shopping or if she had already put it all away.

James did not say anything at first to Sally about this other extraordinary adventure, he was not sure if she would believe him again. James left it until a few hours later they were enjoying their evening meal and drinking a glass of wine. Just as James had expected, Sally was amazed by this tale, but somehow she did seem to believe the story. It was rather too unusual for James to have made up, and why would he? He even had a few blisters as proof of the manual work that he had been doing?

When she had finished hearing the tale Sally stated that "There seems to be something special and rather magical about this cottage, even without your amazing stories, this cottage does somehow feel different." "I certainly feel as if I have my own guardian angel" replied James.

They both spent some time sitting comfortably over the remains of the bottle of wine talking about this special house. James and Sally both felt this house had been waiting just for them, since the previous owners had sadly died. They could not help wonder if the house had been left empty for all this time, just waiting for the two of them to discover it. "Then we were so fortunate that the family of the previous owners had been traced, just at the time when we were wanting to buy it, and we were able to do so quite easily in the end," stated Sally. "It was as if the house was just sat here feeling neglected, waiting for us two to come along and discover it," replied James. "Do you think that it was meant for us two or would anyone else have come along eventually and discovered it?"

The pair of them knew that they would probably never have the answer to that question. They also did not know if this old house had any other surprises for them, but were quite content to wait and to see if anything else, strange or unusual, were to happen.

CHAPTER FIVE

Throughout much of the early part of winter James and Sally spent all their spare time finishing off the work on their house. They decorated the remaining rooms, the rooms they had not had time to do earlier. They eventually reached a point when they knew they had at last finished, and that now just about all of the work on their house was completed.

It was really satisfying knowing they had their home more or less as they wanted. The house did feel quite large for just the two of them but they both hoped that maybe some time, in the not too distant future, they would be able to increase their family. At present though, they first wanted to start saving some money and become more financially stable before they thought about starting a family.

James and Sally held a small family party in their home just a week or so before Christmas to say thank you to family members who had helped with the restoration and also of course to show off their new home now that it was just about finished. James and Sally both felt that it would be a good idea to host a larger party, sometime in the future. A party to which they could invite their friends and other acquaintances from around the village. This party though they decided to leave until the following spring or summer when the weather would be warmer and they hopefully would be able to hold the party outside.

Throughout autumn and into early winter Sally and James had spent many a happy hour at the local pub where they were able to get to know many of the other villagers. If the pub was not too busy the landlord, Dave, was more than happy to spend some time chatting, and filling James and Sally in with all the village gossip. Dave was married to Sharon. It was Sharon who did most of the cooking in the pub. She always seemed to be busy in the kitchen so James and Sally did not see as much of her as they did of her husband.

Dave and Sharon had just one son, Ben, who was away at university for a lot of the time. When Ben was home though he was more than happy to help out in the bar. Ben, like his father was very sociable and always greeted James and Sally warmly whenever they visited the pub or if he saw them around the village.

Sally and James had of course got to know Tony quite well. He lived in a small terraced house on the edge of the village. Tony lived by himself and in his own way he kept his personal life very private. Neither James or Sally had any idea if Tony had any family at all, he never mentioned any. At the same time though, Tony was very friendly and was always keen to help around the village.

Tony seemed very versatile and was able to turn his hand to most things. James had seen him one day sorting out a plumbing problem in the pub and the following day they had heard that he had been helping out on one of the farms.

On this particular occasion, they had heard that Tony had been helping with the milking, James gave a shudder just to think about the time he had nearly also had to help with the milking.

James had not seen Tony since he had had to rescue him for the second time, as an angel, and he did now wonder if he had just dreamt the strange adventures that he had had. It did not seem possible though that he had had two dreams where he had to be rescued by the same angel Antonio, an angel who looked just like Tony, with had the same long wavy hair. James had been back into the old outbuilding since his adventure, but he had not tried the rather strange brick door again, maybe, he thought there may come a day when he just might be tempted to do so.

Another of the regular visitors to The Duck and Cow was Pete who was a farmer and he lived fairly close to Sally and James' cottage. Pete was only able to pop into the pub once or twice a week and never stayed for very long. Sally could not imagine how he had any free time at all, as well as running the farm he was married to Wendy and they had five children, all quite young. Sally had bumped into Wendy one day in the village and had introduced herself to the family. Pete and Wendy's children were Josh who was the oldest at twelve and who went to the nearest secondary school about five miles away. The next in line was Laura who was ten, followed by seven year old twin girls Jessica and Emily. Sally could not imagine how Pete and Wendy could tell the twins apart. Sally herself had had to teach a few sets of twins, but she had always seemed to be able to find some difference so that she did not get them muddled, when it came to Jessica and Emily though Sally could not see any difference in them at all. Lastly came the youngest child, Adam who was only three years old. Sally was amazed at how well Wendy coped looking after five young children as well as helping out on the farm. The whole family though did seem quite resourceful and all of them were always cheerful.

When Sally met up with Wendy and her children they were stood at the village pond feeding the handful of ducks that lived there. It was a day when Sally had managed to be away from work in good time and so was home earlier than usual. Sally was just returning from the post box and she decided to go over to introduce herself. Wendy explained that they were waiting for the school bus to drop Josh off. Wendy had collected Laura, Jessica and Emily from the junior school about a mile away and then they all waited there by the pond for Josh.

"These ducks are certainly well fed by all of us lot" said Wendy with a bit of laugh, "we have to bring some bread with us every day. Josh does not really need someone to meet him off of the bus, but this has become somewhat of a routine." Sally stayed awhile chatting to Wendy and the children and then walked back with them, once Josh had been dropped off, since they lived more or less in the same direction.

Living in the nearest house to James and Sally was another couple called Bill and Christine. Their house was situated at the top of Whisper lane, the small dirt track that led to James and Sally's house. The house, where Christine and Bill lived, was also another large detached house. Bill and Christine were also both teachers and worked at the same secondary school that Josh attended. Sally and James did not know these neighbours too well but had bumped into them a few times in the Duck and Cow.

Sally and James had just about managed to finish the work on their house so that it was all completely ready for Christmas. They had promised Sally's parents some time previously they would spend Christmas with them. As Christmas approached they both felt a bit regretful over this decision. With the house looking so good, more or less just as they wanted it, it did seem a shame they were not able to spend this, their first Christmas together as a married couple, here in their first proper home together.

"Never mind" said James giving Sally a hug, "there will be many more Christmases we can spend together here. Maybe next year we could invite the whole family to join us." "It would also have been good to spend it, just the two of us," answered Sally. James laughed at this, "We do have a whole year in which to decide and you have to admit that this is a lovely big house in which to share Christmas with." Sally knew that James was right, they did have their whole lives ahead of them, and there would be plenty more Christmases in this house. She was fortunate that James was all too happy to be spending Christmas with her parents rather than his own family. James parents had visited when they had held the family party and they had exchanged presents then. Maybe next year they would have a big family Christmas here with both sets of parents invited.

As well as helping James to finish the last minute touches to their house Sally had also been busy with the Christmas shopping. The presents were all bought and wrapped up by 23rd December. They had arranged to go and stay with Sally's parents on Christmas Eve. The evening before this they went to the Duck and Cow for a meal. They did not need much of an excuse to spend an hour or two in the cosy friendly pub. The pub was busier than usual, all of the locals seemed to be there and several of the locals had brought family and friends with them. "This is what we will have to do next year," said James, "we will invite all of our family to stay and then come here to the pub to eat, it will save having to do the shopping and cooking, not to mention all the washing up." "Mmm. I might just be tempted by that idea" replied Sally, with a smile.

The atmosphere in the Duck and Cow was always welcoming but tonight it seemed even more special, almost magical. Dave and Sharon, and more than likely with some help from Ben, had been busy decorating the pub. There was a beautiful, good sized tree in the hall just as you walked in, there was not enough room for the tree in the bar area itself, even here in the entrance there was not that much room to have a huge tree. The bar area though was still tastefully decorated with fairy lights strung across the low ceiling and holly above the fire and around the windows.

It was busy in the pub but luckily, they still managed to get a seat by a small table tucked into a corner. The weather had now turned very cold, James and Sally had walked briskly to the pub in order to try to keep warm. There was quite a biting northerly wind, they had both wrapped up well with warm thick coats, gloves and scarves. Inside the pub though it was different, it was hard to imagine now they had warmed up, that it was so cold outside. There was a roaring open fire ablaze in the hearth. The fire not only kept them all warm it also provided a lovely scent, with the smell of the wood burning. It was still also easy to pick out the delicious aromas coming from the kitchen, Sally could certainly make out the smell of roast pork, this smell was mingling alongside other lovely food smells, possibly also a hint of mince pies.

James and Sally spent a few minutes pondering over the specials board trying to decide what to eat, the choice was very varied and they were both hungry, made even more hungry by the lovely smells drifting from the kitchen. Once they had chosen what to eat, James went to the bar to order the food and to buy drinks for them both. Tony was stood behind the bar and took James order. James also bought Tony a pint and they spent a few minutes chatting until Tony was called away to serve another customer. "No rest for the wicked" said Tony, "it looks as if it is going to be a busy night." James was trying to conjure up an image of a wicked angel, but he could not. It was very hard to remember that

Tony was also an angel, but James was now certain that there really was an angel called Antonio, maybe one of these days they would be able to talk to Tony about the subject of angels, not tonight though, he was too busy.

James and Sally sat for longer than usual in the pub after they had finished eating their meal, it was so lovely and warm, they were both reluctant to go outside again and brave the cold weather. As they sat there in the cosy corner of the Duck and Cow, lingering over their last drink, the atmosphere became quieter as people started to leave and drift off home. James and Sally sat for a little while longer after the last orders had been called finishing their drinks. James commented on the weather, about how cold it had become. "At least the forecast is slightly better for the Christmas weekend, we should have a good drive to your mum and dads tomorrow." Neither James nor Sally saw the rather knowing look that passed between Bob and Tony, who were both now tidying up the bar. It was as if Bob and Tony knew other information about the weather forecast for this village for the Christmas period, they did not choose to share this information though with James and Sally.

James and Sally had planned to finish off the last minute packing and Christmas preparations the following morning before setting off on the short drive to Sally's parents. Neither of them had to go to work, James had managed to get the day off, and Sally was already on holiday, the school where she worked had broken up the previous Friday, therefore they managed a comfortable lie in bed the following morning. Sally was still drifting gently in and out of sleep when James got up to make a cup of coffee. With the aroma of coffee wafting into the bedroom, Sally was able to rouse herself and sat up in bed.

James passed Sally her cup and said" You will never guess what?" "Mmm, no idea" replied Sally still somewhat sleepily. "What won't I guess?" At Sally's reply James opened the curtains. "Wow" said Sally who suddenly became much more alert. "That was certainly not mentioned in the forecast." Overnight there had been a light covering of snow, it certainly did not seem to be bad enough to interfere with any Christmas arrangements but it did look beautiful. Their bedroom overlooked the rather large front garden, with a view of trees beyond their garden. They were not over looked at all. The scene from the window did look just as if it should be on a Christmas card.

They took their time drinking the coffee, both enjoying the luxury of a fairly lazy morning. After a while Sally got up and took a shower before going down to prepare breakfast for the two of them. The kitchen was situated more or less underneath the bedroom and therefore had a very similar outlook. Sally felt ripples of pleasure as she looked out onto this wintry scene. She was now very much looking forward to the Christmas period, even if they couldn't spend the time in their lovely new home, at least they were together.

As Sally went about preparing breakfast the snow started falling again, not too heavy just a light flurry. James came down from his shower and together they sat over a leisurely breakfast. Whilst they were sitting there in the warm kitchen the snow did seem to be getting a bit heavier, but neither of them were particularly concerned. "This snow was not forecast, it surely cannot last for too long? It will have stopped and probably all gone by the time that we will be setting off to your parents," said James, quite optimistically.

They finished breakfast and cleared away the dishes before starting on the last minute preparations. There was not much left to do and with them both working together they were done in just over an hour. They were able to sit with another cup of coffee. "I will make us a bit of a snack to eat shortly, I don't want to turn up at mums hungry, I am sure that she has plenty enough to do already." said Sally, "Once we have had something to eat we may as well set off."

While they had been working they had not thought to pay any more attention to the weather. Now that they had stopped they both glanced outside and were taken aback. The snow had not stopped at all while they had been working, but was now coming down heavier than previously. The snow now appeared to be several inches deep.

James was by now reasonably concerned about the car, he was worried that they could have some difficulty getting it up the track leading from their house to the road. "I will just go and have a look to see what it is like, if I had known we were going to get all this snow, I might have moved the car last night up on to the road, or we maybe should have set off

72

a few hours ago." "While you are checking the car, I will just give mum a ring to see what the weather is like there."

Sally's mum answered the phone after a couple of rings. She seemed surprised. They had had a sharp frost there last night but no snow at all, it did seem strange when they did only live about fifteen miles away. "I will ring back shortly and let you know when we are setting off."

Just as Sally put the phone down James came back into the house. He looked cold and somewhat worried. "The snow is deeper than I had thought. If we are going to leave today we need to set off as soon as possible, as it is the car may struggle to get on to the road." Sally explained that she had rung her mum and they did not have any snow. "I am sure we will be fine as soon as we get out of the village and onto the main road."

Together they loaded the car up with bags they needed for the weekend period, Christmas presents and some food and wine. While they were doing so the snow continued to fall. The sky looked rather dark as if the snow was going to continue for some time yet. It did not take James and Sally very long to put everything they needed into the car.

James sat in the driving seat and then started the engine. The car started without a problem, the problem was the track leading from their house. The situation was made worse because the track actually went up hill, it was just a gentle hill which did not usually cause a problem, but today it did. The snow was getting deeper all the time and to their dismay they found that the car would not move. James managed to drive just a few inches but then the wheels started to spin and they both realised they were stuck and would not be going anywhere soon.

There was no way that they could clear the snow from this track, it would be a huge big task as the track was about a quarter of a mile long, it would just take for ever to do so. They looked at each other as if both were hoping that the other would come up with a solution. After a few minutes of considering just what to do Sally came up with an answer. "Did we not say how good it would be to spend our first Christmas in this house together just the two of us. Well let`s do just that. We will go and visit mum and dad in a few days when the snow has gone, it surely cannot last for too long, and we shall stay here and spend Christmas just the two of us together." James had to agree that it was the best and possibly only solution. Sally`s parents were bound to be disappointed, but under the circumstances there was not much they could do. Sally could have asked her dad to come for them, but she knew he was working. He would probably not be finished for a few hours yet, by then the snow could possibly be even deeper, even the village roads would be treacherous.

They really had no choice but to get on and unload the car again. Once they had finished unpacking Sally investigated the contents of their kitchen. This just confirmed, as Sally had thought, the kitchen was well enough stocked up with food. Even though they had planned to go away Sally had still stocked up with plenty of food for when they came back. This food would now be more than enough to last over the Christmas period. "We won't starve, even if this snow continues for a few more days yet, I think the only thing we don't have is sprouts."

Sally then had to go and phone her mum again. Her mum sounded a little bit bemused at the thought of all the snow, as if she did not really believe Sally. Her mum was disappointed, but fortunately not unduly bothered. They did have other family members visiting, and after all this was only one Christmas, there would be plenty more when they would all be together. "We will have to go into the garden and take a few photos" said Sally to James with a smile when she had finished speaking to her Mum, "just to prove that we really do have this much snow, no one will ever believe us otherwise."

Sally and James did just that once they had had another hot drink. They got wrapped up again in some warm clothing and went out into the garden. James took quite a few photos, not just as proof there really was this much snow, but also he took the photos because everywhere did look so beautiful and special. "Maybe," said Sally, next year we could use these photos and make our own Christmas cards."

Once the camera was safely back inside they spent some time having fun in the snow. They built a good sized snowman before they embarked on a snow ball fight, which James of course won. After about an hour or so they both had glowing cheeks but Sally in particular was now feeling the cold. She went back inside then to have a warm shower and to change out of her rather wet clothes. Once Sally was warm again she was able to think about preparing for the evening meal, the one that she had not been expecting to have to be cooking.

As they went back inside it was still snowing with still no sign that it was ever going to stop, James had another look at the car and the track up to the road and knew they would not have made it. Sally was secretly pleased about this unexpected opportunity to be able to spend Christmas together, just the two of them, but she also felt a bit wistful thinking about her family spending Christmas without her.

The following day was just lovely, being able to wake up in their own home on Christmas morning. It felt so special. Sally had gone to a lot of trouble decorating the house for Christmas and it did now feel good that they were able to spend the festive season here together, even though it was not meant to have been this way. Sally spent some of the day preparing a traditional Christmas dinner for the two of them, she had most of the ingredients that she needed, and knew that they would not go hungry. They of course did not have a turkey but Sally had taken a chicken out of the freezer the day before, when she had realised that she would have to cook their Christmas dinner.

It had snowed some more overnight so there was still no chance they could get the car out of the lane. When it came round to late morning though, the sun had come out and they had not had any more snow for an hour or so. James and Sally were both able to unearth a pair of old wellington boots each, they were still in a storage box down in the cellar, a box they had not yet got round to unpacking. They wrapped up well, put the wellies on and set off for a walk to the Duck and Cow. It was not too easy walking in the fairly deep snow but they both enjoyed the exercise and by the time they reached the pub they had both warmed up.

The pub was not as busy has it had been a couple of evenings ago, but it still had a lovely cosy atmosphere. The open fire was lit and the pub did feel plenty warm enough. Tony was stood at the bar, on the other side of it this time. Today Tony was not needed to help in the pub, they could manage without him. For once also, Sharon was not cooking any food in the pub for customers. Today, they were only serving drinks.

The pub was quiet enough for Bob to manage with some help from Ben. "I thought you two were going away for a few days over Christmas?" asked Tony, he had just a hint of a smile. "That was certainly the plan but we could not get the car on to the road with all the snow" replied James. "Where on earth did all of this snow come from, it was certainly not forecast?" "You can never tell in this part of the world, we do rather seem to have our own climate," replied Tony who did not seem at all surprised there should be this amount of snow. James, once again, could not help wonder at just how many more surprises Marton cum Tiddleworth had to offer them.

The rest of Christmas passed by pleasantly. They did not have any more snow and by Boxing Day evening the snow had started to thaw. James knew that provided they did not have any more snow overnight then he would not have any problems getting the car out the following morning, so he would be able to go back to work.

The weekend after Christmas James and Sally did manage to go and visit her parents and they spent a couple of nights with them, it was rather like having a second Christmas. They took along the photos that they had taken in their garden. Both parents were very surprised at the amount of snow. "How is it possible that you managed to get so much snow at Marton cum Tiddleworth when all we got was just a small flurry on Christmas Eve?"

CHAPTER SIX

One Sunday afternoon towards the end of January, James found himself alone in the house for the first time in a while. Sally had gone out shopping with a few friends from work. There were several tasks he could and probably should have been doing, but once again he felt himself drawn to the old outbuilding in the garden. He had not ventured through into the world of make belief as he and Sally now called this strange land. Sally had never gone beyond the outbuilding, although she was not unduly scared of entering the strange land, she certainly did not like the idea of interfering with something that was so different from their everyday life and one that could not be explained.

James and Sally talked about this strange place from time to time. Sally had said she would prefer for James not go there again. Sally was quite worried that he might have an accident there or he may not be able to return. "Do not worry, "replied James, "I do seem to have my own guardian angel, I am sure he will be able to help again if I do get into difficulty." James though knew that Sally did have a valid point, he was possibly putting himself at risk exploring this strange place. He was aware that Tony may not always be around to help. Still though today, James could not resist returning once more to the land of Marton cum Tiddleworth of one hundred years ago.

James wrapped up warmly for this adventure. It had been very cold over the last few days in Marton cum Tiddleworth though at least it had been dry. They had not had another snow fall since Christmas, but they had woken up to a sharp frost the last few mornings and today in particular the frost was lingering around for quite some time.

James took a torch with him, so he could have another look at the star and moon shape. Neither James nor Sally had been into this old outbuilding for quite some time and James was aware that really one day he would have to come in here to clear away all of the old junk that was just laid there getting dirtier and rustier. He decided that this job would wait until spring, when the weather would be warmer.

James spent a few minutes looking at the star and moon shape on the old strange door before he put his hands on them again and gave them a push. Just like before the brick door gave way and opened out on to the field where James had been before. James paused for a few minutes taking in the sight. Before he ventured further he bent down and placed a piece of wood in the doorway in an effort to jam it open so he would be able to return safely, by himself, to his own world.

James stepped out into this field, moving away from the door and turned his back on it. Here the weather was better than the weather that he had left behind. Out here it felt almost like spring. It was not as warm as it had been when he had been here before, but this spring sunshine, if it really was spring, did feel good.

After a moment or two James turned back to the old brick door. To his dismay the door had shut again without him realising, the piece of wood was nowhere to be seen. James was once more trapped on the outside of his own world. James gave an inward groan, but for the time being there was nothing he could do about it, he may just as well enjoy the experience and hope that eventually Antonio would come to his rescue or maybe this time he could manage to find his own way back home. It would be great if he was able to find his own way back home, then this would mean he could come over and visit this world whenever he liked in the future, without having to rely on Antonio coming to his rescue.

James decided on this visit he wanted to avoid any encounter with any farmers, or come to that, any other person in this world, apart from Antonio. James did not want to put himself in the position of having to help out on the farm again, he gave a shudder at the prospect of milking cows. It was very likely that everyone around here was friendly, but James did not also want to have to explain himself to anyone about who he was or where he came from. With these thoughts James set off, he skirted around the side of the field. There was a small wood conveniently located at the side of the field. In amongst the trees James was able to take some shelter, just in case there was anyone around.

This area was similar to the area surrounding the village of Marton cum Tiddleworth that James was familiar with. There was not a dirt track here as there was leading to his house, just a very small foot path. Apart from this though, the surrounding area did look kind of familiar. James own house, the one he knew so very well, was here in this world and still looked similar, as it did today. There were still fields with crops in all around the house but James could not see any track, apart from the small foot path, leading to the house itself. There was also the difference that here it did appear to be spring and consequently everywhere looked greener and more alive.

James decided to head in the direction of what he knew should be the centre of the village. He had no idea if there was even a village here. If this was the same area that James had left behind in 2005 then the village would be there surely? The village of Marton cum Tiddleworth as James knew, was an old village. James knew it was much older than one hundred years.

James managed to walk the full length of the rather large field without seeing anyone. He kept to the shelter of the trees though, just in case there was someone around. At the far end of this field James could see people, presumably farm labourers working in the adjoining field. James stopped for a while to watch these men at work. He could not help but wonder if any of these men had been around when he had helped out on this farm before. He had no desire though to go over and talk to them, just in case he once again found himself having to help. James, at present was happy just watching from a distance.

James could not tell what these farm labourers were doing, and he did not have enough knowledge of a working farm to be able to tell. These men were too far away for James to be able to see them at work properly. James had never previously spent any time on a farm.

After James had dawdled there for quite a while, longer than he had intended, he carried on with his walk so he could explore some more of this village. James could not stay here too long in this world, he wanted to be back at home for when Sally returned. He did not wish for Sally to be worried. James had not thought to bring his mobile phone with him, but that was silly, there was no way he would be able to get a signal here! Perhaps though, next time he came visiting this area via the old outbuilding he would bring his mobile phone just to try it out, of sheer curiosity, to see if it was at all possible to use the phone here.

James carried on in the direction that he felt should bring him very shortly to the village and yes he was right. He could see not too far in front of him, the village green with the same small pond just to one side. James stopped in his tracks. So far he had been able to find good shelter amongst trees that grew in between the fields along the short walk to the village centre. Now though upon reaching the centre of the village there was an unfortunate shortage of trees and nowhere for James to hide.

James stayed where he was for a while in the cover of the trees. From where he was standing James could see quite a lot of village life. The village looked busier here than it did in the village that James was now familiar with. Even the duck pond seemed to have more activity, there must be twice as many ducks here than James had ever previously noticed.

James was stood at the edge of the village green. The duck pond was to the left of him and in front of him at the other end of the village green was the main hub of the village, the main hub being the village pub. This pub was similar to the one James knew, the one which he was now quite familiar with but this one was definitely livelier. There were a lot more people milling around this pub. The building was obviously the same, but it had been altered possibly once or twice over the course of time. James could just about make out the name of the pub, this had obviously not changed over the last one hundred years. James wondered how long the pub had been there and if it was always called the Duck and Cow. The pub was now open and it did indeed look very busy.

James attention was drawn to a building to the left hand side of his view, some way beyond the duck pond. James recognised this building. In the village that James knew, this was a rather grand detached house. James did not know the present occupiers very well, just well enough to say hello on the odd occasions he had come across them in the Duck and Cow. James could see though that one hundred years ago this building was not used as a house. This building was not in use in 2005 as it once had been. James could see that the original purpose of the building was that of a school. The house James knew was reasonably large but here as a school building, it seemed to be relatively small.

This school was not open today, it all appeared to be quiet. James though could just make out the name of the school. The school was simply called Marton cum Tiddleworth junior and infant school. James presumed this school was just for the younger children and perhaps the older children went to a larger school situated presumably somewhere out of the village, as they also did in 2005. The village had never obviously been large enough to sustain its own secondary school. James wondered how long ago the small school had closed, and presumed there must have come a time when it was no longer viable to keep such a small school open, or maybe for some other reason the building had become no longer suitable for purpose.

James could also make out the purpose of another building in this village of 1905. This building, which was also next to the Duck and Cow, but on the other side away from the school. In the village that James knew this was also a rather large detached house and it still looked again, quite similar to how it had done originally. James could clearly see that the original purpose of this building was that of a blacksmiths. It was also presumably a Sunday in this village as well as in 2005, and so today the blacksmiths shop was shut.

James decided that he would really like to visit this village again on a week day so he could see more activity. There was quite a lot of activity going on today, but James was now curious enough to wish to return, on a day when the blacksmiths and the school were both open. He knew he would just have to wait until he was able to take a day off work. James knew that Sally would also be curious to see this old school, to be able to compare it to the school where she worked, but it may not be possible. James doubted if he would ever be able to persuade Sally to come and join him on one of these adventures.

James had been standing in the shadow of the trees for quite some time. He took a few tentative steps forward and ventured out onto the village green itself. James stood there for a while longer just on the edge of the green, well away from anyone else. He did not want to draw any attention to himself. Not that far from James there was a group of children playing a game together, they did not take any notice of him, they were all too engrossed in their play.

While James had been standing there he noticed a couple of men standing not too far away, talking outside the "Duck and Cow." Both men had a pint of beer each. James was so envious, he was thirsty as he had now been away from home for longer than he had intended. He was ready for a drink and could so easily have managed a pint of beer. Of course though there was no way that he could walk into the pub and buy himself a drink, not with the change he had in his pocket. He wondered if he would ever be able to acquire some money from this period of time, so he would be able to come back one day and buy himself a drink. That though was perhaps just wishful thinking.

James was aware he had probably been sitting on the edge of the village green for the best part of an hour, he knew that he really should be heading off back home. He still had to find out how he was going to actually get back home.

Just as James was getting up to go, two men who were walking in the direction of the pub bid James good day. They mentioned that they had not seen James around here before. "No", replied James, "I am just passing through, and had just stopped off for a rest." "Well good day to you then" answered one of the men and with that they headed off towards the pub. James stared over wistfully to the pub before he set off in the opposite direction and headed towards home.

James passed several other villagers on his way home, he was not as discreet on his way back. James just nodded at these villagers and smiled, he did not wish to engage in conversation with any of these people, just in case they were curious and wanted to know where James had come from. He was well aware that his accent alone was different and would make him stand out.

James did not know how he was going to get home, how he was once again going to travel forward one hundred years, but he just had this feeling that somehow or other he would manage. He could not rely on Antonio every time he wanted to time travel, and he knew that he would want to time travel again.

James walked on in the general direction of where his house should be, and without too much trouble James did indeed find his house. When James had set out on this adventure about two hours or so ago he had gone through the shed and then had found himself on one side of a very high wall, James once more found this wall, he walked along the wall, which did lead him to his house.

The house was very similar to the way it was in the present day, but in this house there was no garden. The house as it was one hundred years before James lived there, just gave way to fields. There was a high wall at the back of the house that James occupied in 2005 but it did not seem to be as high as this wall that ran along the back of the house in 1905.

James walked slowly along past this wall, and then along towards the house. As James was walking, he was pondering on just what he should do. He could not just enter this house, although to all intent and purpose it was his house, but to enter now would be to trespass and it would not take James to his own time period. James was jingling the key to his own house which had been sat in the pocket of his jeans. The door on this house in 1905 and his house were different, the door had obviously been changed over the course of time.

James knew he could not just stand there forever waiting for the answer to his problem. Previously the answer to this problem of how to return to his own world had been resolved in the old barn. So once again James decided to try this barn. James did not wish to keep on relying on Tony, or Antonio, every time he came to visit this world but at present he could not think of any other option.

James walked back slowly along the outside of the wall in the general direction of the barn. While he was walking James glanced down and saw something that he had not noticed before. This entire wall was made of the same uniform design of brick, but now James noticed a slight anomaly in part of the brick wall. Near the bottom of the wall, part way along it there was a slight change. James stooped down to have a closer look. There were several bricks missing from this one small part of the wall. These bricks had been replaced by a flagstone, and this flagstone had the same design on it that James was becoming familiar with, that of a star and a crescent moon. It was surprising that James had managed to spot it, it was low down on the wall, and it didn't particularly stand out. Over a period of time it had also weathered, making it a bit harder to spot.

James reached down, and out of instinct, pressed on to this flagstone. He certainly didn't need to use much force, but to his amazement part of the wall opened up before him. This opening was the same size and shape as the doorway that James had used to enter into this world not that long ago. James peered around the doorway and then took a tentative step forward. He found himself once more back in the old outbuilding and he knew once more he was back home. James was so relieved to have got back safely home and also to have done so without any help from Tony, although the previous ride back home on the back of the angel had been very exciting.

When James went back inside the house, he found that Sally had not yet arrived home, James realised this was perhaps fortunate as it would stop Sally worrying about him exploring the village of one hundred years ago. James made himself a cup of tea and then put the kettle back on ready to make Sally a drink as he knew it would probably not be too long before she was home.

Sally did arrive home when James was only half way through his cup of tea. Sally was full of gossip after spending the day with friends and she shared much of this with James before asking him how his day had been. James did look somewhat sheepish when Sally asked him this question, as he knew that she did not really approve of his time travelling. James though did tell Sally about his expedition to the Marton cum Tiddleworth of one hundred years ago.

Although Sally did not approve at all of James travelling back in time, she was still curious about his experience. Sally rather liked the idea of the village school and felt that it was a shame it had had to close. "Perhaps you will have to come with me some time to look for yourself" "Maybe, I might just do so one day, but not just yet, I would need to feel confident that it was completely safe first." replied Sally. She looked a bit thoughtful though as if she just one day might be tempted. James knew better than to keep on about this, Sally may make up her mind one day, but James still was not sure how safe he himself was by venturing back through time, he certainly did not want to put Sally into any danger.

CHAPTER SEVEN

In March James parents came to spend a weekend with James and Sally. They had visited Marton cum Tiddleworth once or twice before, previously though it had been when they had come to help with the restoration work on the house. This time though James parents, Fred and Diana had come more to spend time with the young couple, and to relax, rather than just for the purpose of working on the house. Fred and Diana lived about fifty miles away so they did not have the chance to visit too often. They also both worked full time. This was the first time they were both able to come to stay for a full weekend at the cottage. They had not been to visit since all of the work on the house had been finished, so they were very impressed when they arrived on the Friday evening and had a guided tour of the property.

On the Saturday Sally and Diana went off to visit the nearby town to do some shopping. Fred was not too keen on joining the girls on a shopping trip, so instead he offered to help James in the garden. James showed his dad the few unusual flagstones they had come across dotted around the property and mentioned that they had planned to move them and re-lay them on the lawn at the front of the house. "Since they are rather unusual we thought that they would be quite eye catching, it seems a shame they have gone unnoticed for so long." Fred had to agree with his son that they would look good on the lawn and offered to help James move the flagstones.

James and Fred first of all tried to lift the flagstone that Sally had discovered at the back of the house. It was more of a struggle than they had expected to loosen it from the ground, but they did eventually manage to do so. "This one must have been here for as long as the house," commented Fred who was feeling a bit puffed from the exertion. Between them they did manage to eventually lift it out and carry it to the front of the house in an old wheelbarrow that James had found in the shed. They put the flagstone in place and went to dig out the next one.

The next one was not so far away. This one was already situated in the front garden, but again it had gone unnoticed for a long time. This flagstone had also been covered in weeds before it had been discovered. Sally had also discovered it when she was clearing the path that ran along the side of the house. This flagstone, like the other one, also proved to be a struggle for the two men to lift, but they did eventually manage to put it in place near to the other one that they had moved. The plan was to lay out the flagstones so that they formed a path down the middle of the lawn. Since these two flagstones had taken much more effort than they had anticipated, the two of them agreed very easily to stop for a while and have a drink. They were both quite surprised that it was now lunch time. James went to collect a couple of beers from the fridge and also made a few sandwiches for them both to share.

When they had started moving the flagstones it had been a pleasant, warm day. Neither of them had taken too much notice of the weather while they had been working. When James returned to the garden he became aware of just how much the weather had changed. James was surprised as he had taken notice of the weather forecast, it was supposed to be a good weekend, but now the sky looked rather dark, as if it could rain at any moment. Fred was still outside, pulling out a few weeds from one of the flower beds when James approached with lunch. "I think maybe we should take these back inside," commented James, "Have you seen the colour of that sky."

James and Fred had intended to spend more time that afternoon moving flagstones, it had initially seemed to be a relatively easy task, one they both thought they would manage to achieve in just a couple of hours. Over lunch though James put the television on and before long they were both engrossed in a football match. It didn`t take much persuasion for them both to call it a day in the garden and to rest and watch the football for a while. Fred offered to perhaps help move another stone the following morning before they had to leave. James had also been wondering if Tony would also be able to help to move the others, probably not tomorrow, he could well be helping out at the pub, but maybe the following weekend.

While Sally and Diana had been out shopping, the weather had also for them been pleasantly warm and sunny. It was not until they were driving back and were just a few miles from home that they both noticed the dark cloud ahead of them. The dark cloud seemed to be just sitting right over Marton cum Tiddleworth. "Great," said Sally, "that rather ominous looking cloud seems to be sitting directly over home. I had been planning to do a barbecue this evening, since it has been unseasonably warm."

"There is no rain forecast" commented Diana, "it will probably have blown away by the time that we come to eat." "I guess so" replied Sally, "if not we can always just have the meal inside instead, if we find that it is not going to be warm enough to be sat outside eating."

When they arrived back at James and Sally's house, the cloud had not moved. All of Marton cum Tiddleworth did indeed seem to be caught under this rather dark cloud. Sally decided not to risk lighting the barbecue but cooked the meal she had planned indoors, and they ate inside instead. It was just as well they made this decision. Just as they were about to start eating the first of the raindrops fell. Only a few minutes later the rain was coming down really heavily. "The weathermen seemed to have got the weather forecast wrong this time" commented Fred. "The weather was supposed to be fine all weekend."

It did not dampen their spirits though. The four of them sat for some time around the dining table. They lingered for awhile after they had finished eating watching the rain lashing down. "Hopefully it won't last too long, we may still be able to have that walk tomorrow." They had been planning to have a walk around the surrounding area finishing the walk off, of course, at the Duck and Cow. The four of them wanted to have Sunday lunch there before Fred and Diana had to leave. James and his Dad were also hoping to shift that other flagstone.

The following morning the rain had stopped, but it was quite grey looking, the sky was still very dark as if there was more rain to come. The garden was now very soggy. James and Fred did not bother trying to move any more flagstones. "They have been in place for so long, another weekend or so will not make much difference. When we are at the pub I can ask Tony, if he is there, if he could maybe give me a hand with them sometime."

Instead of gardening and walking, they had a lazy Sunday morning. A light leisurely breakfast followed by several cups of coffee. It gave the four of them further opportunity to have a good natter and to catch up with all of their news. They did set off from the house late morning and managed to go on a much shorter walk then they had originally planned. The walk just took them around the village of Marton cum Tiddleworth itself. Fred and Diana had not really been into the village before, they had only seen parts of it as they had driven directly to Sally and James house. They were both pleasantly surprised by the village, by just how picturesque it was. They were also quite taken aback by the grandeur of many of the houses in the village and also by the fact that all of the houses in the village were so old, there were no new properties at all.

As they were walking round James pointed out to Sally the house that had at one time been the local school. They had both presumed that it had always been just a house, but now that they looked at it more closely they could both picture it as a rather small quaint village school. James managed to point out the school just to Sally, he had no intention of telling his parents about his time travelling, James did not think that they would believe him, and if by any chance they did believe him, they would, understandably, be very concerned about his safety.

They finished their shortened walk just where they intended, at the Duck and Cow. They stopped there for a while and had lunch before Fred and Diana set off back to their home. Both of James parents were also impressed by the pleasant atmosphere of the pub and by the very tasty home cooking. James and Sally were able to introduce them to several of the locals, though Tony was not in the pub today. One of the main topics of conversation around the bar that lunch time was of the sudden change in the weather and just how much it had changed. "Never mind" said Fred "it has not stopped us enjoying our weekend here." Shortly after lunch Fred and Diana had to leave but promised to be back again before too long.

CHAPTER EIGHT

The following weekend James was out tidying up in the front garden, he had begun to realise that the weeding was a never ending job, however this was of course an inevitable task with having such a large garden. As James was bent down over one of the flower beds he became aware of someone approaching. He looked up to see Tony. James was only too pleased for an excuse to stop for a while, just as his back was beginning to ache with the constant bending down. "Hello" greeted James warmly, "do you have time to stop for a cup of coffee?" "That would be great" replied Tony, "though I don't want to interrupt you if you are busy." "No problem, I could do with a cup myself and would welcome the break, Sally will be glad of the company."

The weather had not improved at all since the previous weekend. There seemed to have been a dark cloud that had descended over Marton cum Tiddleworth ever since then. They had not had a great deal of rain but this dark cloud remained with them. It was strange but James and Sally could not help notice that whenever they left the village the weather seemed to improve quite considerably, but there was always that dark cloud waiting for them when they got back home again. Now though that it was the end of March they were both optimistic that the weather was bound to get better soon.

Today though James and Tony headed inside for the cup of coffee, it was too cold to be stood outside for any length of time. Sally joined them and the three of them sat for a while around the kitchen table. After ten or fifteen minutes the subject of the weather did come up. Sally asked Tony if Marton cum Tiddleworth really did have its own climate. "The weather here does seem to be different from the weather that they are having just beyond the village. Mostly the weather here has been good since we first moved to the village, but there was all that snow over Christmas that only affected Marton cum Tiddleworth and now we have this dark cloud over head that does not seem to be moving."

"I must agree," replied Tony, "we are usually quite lucky, the weather in Marton cum Tiddleworth does usually tend to be favourable. The last time though that we were this unfortunate with the weather was quite a while ago, when the previous occupants of this house decided to move things around in the garden. No one knew why it should make a difference, but they decided to change the position of some of the flagstones and for a few weeks after that the weather here was really bad with an amazing amount of rain." "It was of course many years ago but at the time it really was the topic of conversation in the village and some of the older residents still remember it."

James looked surprised at this, it had to be an amazing coincidence. James though felt compelled to confess, that he and his dad had also decided to alter the flagstones. "They are so unusual that we wanted to make more of a feature of them on the front lawn." "I don't wish to sound too superstitious" replied Tony "but would you mind very much if they were moved back into their original position?" James thought about this just for a few moments and said that it did not matter too much if they were returned to their original place. "We certainly wouldn't wish to be responsible for inflicting this weather on Marton cum Tiddleworth right through spring and summer. The only problem is, it did take a lot of effort to move them in the first place. It could be really back breaking moving them back again, it would certainly be worthwhile giving it a go though if we are able to move this dark cloud away from the village."

Tony of course offered to help. "If you are not too busy we could make a start right now." Tony suggested that they could just try moving one of the flagstones that afternoon and then leave the other couple for another day if indeed it did prove to put too much strain on their backs. There was no time like the present so they both got up and headed into the garden. James got out a spade he hoped they would be able to use to lift the flagstone with and a wheelbarrow so that they could transport it easily. James had expected the flagstone to move a bit easier than it had when he and his dad had moved it previously, since this time it had not been laid in one place for very long. This time though the flagstone with some effort from both of them, lifted out of place relatively easily, surprisingly so, and it also felt lighter as they lifted it into the wheelbarrow.

It seemed to take no time at all before they had replaced this first flagstone and returned it to the patch of bare ground that had been left exposed. Neither of them needed any persuasion to carry on and to reposition the other two flagstones. James knew that it would be no problem to find an alternative feature for the large lawn at the front of the house. These flagstones though had probably been here for a very long time and if this was the correct position for them to be, then it did not really matter.

In the future, James would make sure all of the garden was always kept tidier, by doing so, they would be able to see these unique flagstones, wherever they were positioned. James was very pleased he and his dad had not got too carried away last weekend and decided to move the flagstone from the cellar as well, as James had been planning to do.

James and Tony both stood back to look at the last flagstone after it had been returned. James felt his back ache a little but nothing like as much as it had done previously, he knew that a long soak in a hot bath later on would help. As they stood there James suddenly glanced up and became aware of the weather. He had not noticed that it had changed, but now for the first time in what seemed like quite some time, although it was in actual fact only a week, the sun was shining and it felt several degrees warmer already. James could not believe this change had occurred just because of a few flagstones.

Sally came outside just then with a tray of tea and biscuits. She was also surprised at how quickly they had replaced the flagstones and was also pleasantly surprised to see the sun was now shining. Sally just felt this was all really too much of a coincidence. Sally asked of Tony, "is there anything else we need to know about this garden, or come to that the house itself? I would not like to think that we could not make any further changes in the future, if we felt like it, without disturbing the balance of nature"

Tony reassured them that while the flagstones remained in this position it was unlikely any other changes they chose to make would make any other difference. "I can honestly say I do not know what it is about these flagstones, perhaps" he said with a bit of a laugh, "it should be written into the deeds of the house that these flagstones should not be moved again."

"We are intending to stay in this village for many years," replied James rather more seriously than Tony, "maybe we must remember to pass this information on to any future occupants of this house, though I do not know how we would explain the reason why."

Spring, once the flagstones had been moved, arrived in good time in Marton cum Tiddleworth. There seemed to be such an abundance of spring flowers, snowdrops, daffodils and crocuses. All of these flowers could be seen on the village green, in many gardens, including James and Sally's, and also on the grass verges running alongside the country lanes. In the woods surrounding the village there was also an abundance of bluebells, from a distance the bluebells stood out as though it were a carpet of luxuriant blue.

James and Sally still took many walks around the surrounding countryside, they never got tired of the scenery. Neither of them could get over the abundance of all these beautiful spring flowers. They could not decide between them if they had just not taken that much notice before of spring flowers anywhere, or if there was an unusually large crop of wild flowers this year. Was it simply because they were now in Marton cum Tiddleworth and this village would never cease to amaze and delight them.

One particular Sunday afternoon in early April the sun did feel lovely and warm. James and Sally set off on what was to be a good long walk, making a large circle of the village. They took a blanket and a picnic with them. After walking several miles they found themselves in a lovely spot, somewhere they had not come across before, even though it was not that far out of the village.

They had been walking through a wood and right in the middle of the wood they came across a clearing. The clearing was large and was carpeted with a lush green grass. It seemed like a good time and place to stop for a break. James spread out the blanket to one side of this clearing and Sally took out the picnic from the bag. By now they were both feeling hungry and very greedily tucked into the picnic of salad, bread, cheese and fruit. Sally had also packed a small bottle of wine as well as some juice.

Sally and James had only been sat there picnicking for only a few minutes enjoying the food, when Sally gave James a nudge and silently pointed out a family of rabbits not too far from where they were sitting. They then spotted what they thought was another rabbit rushing across the clearing, but soon realised that this was too large for a rabbit and it was in fact a hare.

Soon after seeing the hare James looked towards the far end of the clearing and saw standing, just by the trees, two rather majestic looking deer. He once again pointed these out silently to Sally, not wishing to make a sound for fear of scaring them off. They both sat entranced for some time watching them. Neither James nor Sally had seen deer before in the wild. The deer did wander off after some time, but James and Sally had felt that it was another magical moment, just being able to sit there and watch the rather enchanting wildlife.

Having now finished the picnic, James and Sally lay down on the blanket. The sun still felt pleasantly warm on their skin and they both fell, not quite asleep, but into that pleasant drowsy state where they were so easily able to day dream, mainly about their so contended life in Marton cum Tiddleworth.

James was day dreaming about the Marton cum Tiddleworth of one hundred years ago and was wondering when he would get the opportunity to visit the old village again, and if he would ever get to sample the beer in that Duck and Cow, or maybe to ride on the back of an angel again. Sally was dreaming about a time in the future when they would be able to share walks like this with one or maybe two children, they would also have to bring a ball along, one they could play with on this lovely grassy area.

James and Sally both roused from their day dreaming at about the same time. It was still only April and this pleasant warm day could not last for ever. The sun had now disappeared behind a large dark cloud and they both now sat up with a bit of a shiver. Together they tidied away the remnants of their picnic and headed back towards home. The rest of the walk home did not take too long but both felt very relaxed for the opportunity to have spent this time outside.

CHAPTER NINE

On the following Saturday afternoon James was once again out in the front garden. He never did get any more weeding and tidying done in the garden on the previous Saturday, when he had found himself shifting flagstones, and once again he made another start on this task. James had spent about half an hour or so weeding and seemed to be making good progress when Tony came along again. James knew he could have done with the time to carry on tidying up the garden, but it was also very easy to find an excuse to stop and talk just for a few minutes.

They greeted each other and spent a few minutes talking about the improved weather. Then Tony nodded his head in the direction of the old outbuilding. "Have you managed to get that cleared out yet?" "I keep meaning to give it a good tidy and clear some stuff out" replied James "One of these days the extra storage space may come in handy, but it does seem a shame to throw away other people's property." "Can I have a nosey in there?" requested Tony. "No problem" replied James, "did you know the previous couple well? If there is anything in there that you would like you are welcome to it, maybe a keepsake or something."

They both wandered over to the old outbuilding together. It was not locked James has started to use one of the shelves as somewhere to keep his few gardening tools. "Strange door" commented James nodding his head towards the back of the shed. Tony gave a strange smile, "have you by any chance tried to open it?" James had not wanted to tell Tony that yes, not only had he worked out how to open the door but that he had also been through the door and done some exploring on the other side. Now though that Tony had brought up the subject he did confess to him that he was now well aware of what lay on the other side of this door.

James told Tony about the excursion that he had had through the door a few weeks previously and how he had enjoyed the wander around the village. "It would have been great fun and was so tempting to go and have a drink in the pub, but it was not possible to do so. I didn't have the correct money on me to buy a pint."

"Shall we go across there now?" asked Tony. James was quite taken aback by this suggestion but was certainly not going to refuse. "I will just let Sally know I am going out, just so that she does not come looking for me!"

James popped back into the house to let Sally know he was just going to the Duck and Cow with Tony. Sally was not unduly bothered and fortunately did not ask to come along. James kind of omitted to tell her they were going for a pint in the Duck and Cow of one hundred years ago. Sally right then, was busy in the kitchen, she was just starting to prepare the evening meal, she told James to let Tony know he was more than welcome to join them. "OK thanks, we won't be too long."

The old outbuilding was out of sight from where Sally was busy, preparing food in the kitchen, so she was not able to see that James and Tony had headed in here rather than up the track and into the village in the conventional way. In the outbuilding Tony was pottering around looking at some of the junk that had laid dormant in there for some time.

"Did Sally not want to join us then?" asked Tony with a grin. "Fortunately not, she is aware of the time travelling I have been doing, but does not approve, she is naturally a bit worried about it. One of these days though, you never know, she may join me, but not just yet. By the way Sally did say you are more than welcome to join us for dinner, she will be cooking plenty for the three of us."

Tony opened up the door, James realised he had probably been this way many times before, perhaps when the previous owners lived in this cottage. Together they entered the world of Marton cum Tiddleworth of one hundred years ago. The sunshine here was a little bit brighter and it also felt a degree or two warmer. James wanted to know so much about this world but did not wish to bombard Tony with too many questions, he guessed and really hoped there would be plenty of time in the future to really get to know this land.

They walked together towards the Duck and Cow. On the way they came across a lady who was just leaving the school building. Tony stopped to talk to her for a few minutes and introduced her to James. This lady turned out to be the village school teacher, she was in fact, the only teacher in the small village school. The lady was called Christine, and she seemed to be very pleasant. As they were stood talking James learned that Christine was married to another teacher who taught at the grammar school just a few miles away. When Christine mentioned that her husband was called William he could not help but give a small gasp, which neither Christine nor Tony appeared to have noticed. James did not like to ask, in front of Christine, if this was just a coincidence that in 2005 there was another couple living in Marton cum Tiddleworth with the exactly the same names and same occupations.

Although it was a Saturday Christine had just called in at the school to do a bit of marking and tidying up. "It is easier than carrying the slates home that these children use to write on." They said goodbye to Christine and carried on towards the pub. Tony talked about Christine and her husband and mentioned the house where they lived, of course it had to be the same one where Chris and Bill were living in 2005. "That seems quite a coincidence," mentioned James. "You are right there, we do seem to have a lot of coincidences in this village," replied Tony. James did not comment on this any further, he could not help feel there were perhaps a few more secrets hidden in this village he and Sally had yet to discover and possibly even many more that they would never get to find out about.

Although James had mentioned he would have liked to visit this Duck and Cow and Tony had suggested they make this journey, it had somehow not occurred to James that they would actually be visiting the pub for a drink, until they got very close to it. He had presumed they would just be wandering around the village, as he had done recently by himself. Just before they entered the pub James stopped and said that if they did go inside, which he really wanted to do, he had no way of buying a pint. "Don't worry" replied Tony, "I am sure that farmer Ted will be in the pub and I do happen to know that he owes you a pint." At first it did not occur to James what Tony meant by this statement, and then it dawned on him, farmer Ted must be the farmer that James had spent a couple of hours working for, and Tony was certainly right, he did owe him at least one pint.

The Duck and Cow had of course been modernised and altered over the last one hundred years, but there were still many of the features which did not seem to have changed too much. There was no need for a fire in the pub today, it was too warm, but there was still an open fire here in the same place and looking very similar to the one in the modern day pub. The bar was also in the same place and James could not decide if this was the same piece of wood that the counter was made from. Was it possible that one piece of wood had been in the same place for over one hundred years? James knew that there were a lot of questions he would have liked to ask, but this was not the right time

Stood, propping up the bar was the farmer Tony had mentioned, and was indeed the same one James had worked for. Farmer Ted greeted Tony very warmly, they seemed to be old friends. Tony introduced James, and Ted did buy them both a very welcome pint of beer. The beer tasted differently to what James was expecting. He sipped slowly at first, somewhat cautiously, as if he did not know what to expect. This beer was warmer than any that he drunk before, but it seemed to have more flavour, with certainly a stronger flavour of hops. This pint was definitely not unpleasant. James felt that he could very easily get used to this beer.

As they were talking the farmer happened to mention his family. It was mainly Ted and Tony who were doing the talking, James was too busy taking in the surroundings, and of course enjoying and savouring his pint. It turned out though farmer Ted also had five children and this included a set of twins, another coincidence?

James was half way down his pint and very much enjoying the atmosphere in the pub when the bar man cursed and mentioned that the beer had run out, the barrel needed changing. The bar man was working by himself and there were several customers waiting impatiently to be served. Tony offered to go down into the cellar to change the barrel. "Thanks" came the response, "it would be good of you." James asked if he could also go down into the cellar, he was really keen to see as much as he could of life of one hundred years ago. Tony did not mind, but warned him to be careful of the steps, "they are not very even and the lighting is very poor"

Down in the cellar, the floor was covered in flagstones, these did feel a bit sticky. Even down here in the dim light,

James was still able to pick out two flagstones which were different from the others, but to James they now looked so familiar. These two flagstones also had a star and crescent moon on them.

James pointed these flagstones out to Tony, who James realised, must have already known they were here. Tony had obviously been in this cellar many times before, he certainly appeared to be very familiar with it. James could not help wonder how much time Tony spent in this particular village, but he was reluctant to pry.

James would have loved to have stayed there longer not just looking for more of these flagstones but just taking in the sights of this old beer cellar, not to mention the rather grand smell of the beer. In the short time James had been looking at the floor, Tony had managed to sort out the barrel so the beer was flowing once more up in the bar. The two of them returned up the rather uneven and worn steps and back into the bar itself so they could finish their pints. James had thought the bar itself had been very dim when they had first entered it, but now after the very poor light down in the cellar he found that he was blinking as the light did now appear to be quite bright.

Unfortunately for James it did not take them too much longer to finish their drinks and then they had to leave, it was time for them to be heading off for home. James very much hoped he would have the chance to visit this pub again, during this period of time.

On the walk back home they naturally had to talk about the village and the strange flagstones. James very much wanted to know just why these flagstones kept appearing and if there was any significance behind them. "You are obviously quite well aware by now that this is a rather unusual village," commented Tony. "You are not kidding," replied James. Tony went on to say, "most folk in the village are very much aware this village is different, though I am lucky enough to have a little more insight than most others about the strange occurrences. Many of the villagers who have lived here a long time just accept the village as it is, the children who are born in to this village never question why this village is that bit different. You and Sally are slightly unusual, it has been a long time since anyone new came to live in the village. Even I though do not know the reason behind the star and moon flagstones, why they keep appearing in the village. I am only aware they do all have to be kept in equilibrium. You have by now worked out if the flagstones are moved, then it does seem to be at the detriment to the rest of the village."

"There was an occasion several years ago when a beer barrel was dropped rather carelessly in the Duck and Cow onto the stone floor in the cellar. It was just an accident, it had been Dave who had dropped it. He is very used to handling the barrels and no one knew what happened this time but as a result Dave injured his back and was off work sick for two or three months.

The barrel landed onto one of these rather unique flagstones. Fortunately the flagstone was not damaged but it felt at the time as if there was a minor earth tremor in Marton cum Tiddleworth. Everyone in the village felt the ground judder. It is just possible, though we will never know, if the barrel had instead landed on any other ordinary flagstone, than the injury Dave received would not have been anywhere as serious. It would also not have felt as if we were having a small earthquake."

At one time James would have been tempted not to believe this story, but he was now beginning to wonder that probably anything could happen here in this magical and mysterious village. He made a mental note to himself to ensure these unusual flagstones on his property were always well looked after.

When they arrived back at Whisper Lane, Sally was just putting the finishing touches to their evening meal. As they sat down to eat, Sally asked by way of conversation if the pub had been busy. "Not too bad," replied James. James and Tony glanced at each other, neither of them wanted to bring up the subject of time travelling. Tony was aware of Sally's concern regarding James desire to travel back in time one hundred years, and he respected her judgement, he therefore chose to leave this subject well alone.

While they were sitting around the table eating, James could not help but wonder to himself if Sally would ever have the courage to venture into the world of one hundred years ago so they would be able to share the experience together. Tony was also thinking similar thoughts, but Tony was aware maybe one day, in the not too distant future it was more than likely Sally would be persuaded to cross the boundary between the two worlds. Tony had really come to like both James and Sally and for the time being he did not wish to do anything to upset this friendship by encouraging Sally to do something that so obviously did trouble her.

Sally had really excelled herself with this meal, the food was delicious and there was certainly plenty of it. Feeling rather full, the three of them worked together to clear the table. Sally enjoyed having Tony round as he really was quite interesting, he was also always helpful, and always made himself at home.

Once the dishes were tidied away James made coffee which they drank in the lounge. They sat for a few minutes in a companionable silence before Tony brought up a new subject. Tony announced that he had a suggestion to make. "The couple who used to live here before, Mr and Mrs Walker, used to host a party every year for all the villagers. It was an annual event and took place in your garden on midsummer's eve. Last year the village did still hold this event, but it was not the same." Tony stopped talking then and paused for a while. James and Sally knew he was dropping a great big hint. He was obviously wanting them to carry on the tradition with the Midsummers Eve party.

"We had been thinking of hosting maybe a barbecue in the summer for family and friends to say thank you to all those who have helped with the house. We had never thought though of inviting all of the village." Tony went on to explain about the times when Mr and Mrs Walker had held this party previously. "There were usually about one hundred guests who attended, they were all just from the village itself. If you would like to continue with this tradition, then I can assure you that you will have plenty of support. Everyone will help out. The only thing you two will have to do is to provide your garden for the evening." Tony stopped talking for a while to let this plan sink in with James and Sally.

"The pub always closes its doors just for this one evening, on midsummers eve. The pub is open every other night of the year." Tony went on to explain. James interrupted at this, "What if they have customers who want to come to the pub on this particular evening from outside the village?" Tony gave a shrug, "There may well be quite a few people who are disappointed, however, it is only closed for this one evening, they never seem to lose any regular customers over this."

Tony went on to explain that Dave with help from Sharon and Ben would set up a bar in their garden. They would bring along a selection of beer, lager and wine, as well as a plentiful supply of non-alcoholic drinks. They would of course supply the glasses as well, usually plastic ones to avoid any broken glass. Everyone tends to bring some food along as well, it is like one huge faith supper. As well as food all the villagers provide their own plates, cutlery, chairs or a blanket to sit on the floor. There is never any washing up to do and very little mess to clear away afterwards. Everyone in the village would just love, with of course your permission, to borrow the garden again for the evening.

James and Sally looked at each other. They both knew they could not refuse, and they also knew that it would help to establish themselves well and truly into village life. More or less speaking at the same time they both gave their blessing to Tony to go ahead with the party. "Please though" asked Sally, "Do let us know if there is anything that we can do to help."

CHAPTER TEN

The day of the party seemed to be upon them so soon. The party had always been held on midsummers eve, despite which day of the week that this fell on, or what the weather forecast was. Tony insisted they could not break this tradition. On the day of the party, both Sally and James were pleasantly pleased to see Tony was quite right, they did not have to put in any effort at all into the planning and preparations for this party.

Sally did some baking for the occasion, but soon realised on the evening of the party there was more than enough food at the party, without her contribution. A long table had appeared in their garden earlier on in the day, they found out later it was Tony and Ben who had brought it over and set it up. All the food was placed on this table and before long there was a huge feast laid out before them. The last time Sally had seen this amount of food had been at their wedding.

By early evening couples and families started to arrive, most of these people James and Sally now knew by sight. James and Sally had both been busy at work all day, and had then been inside getting ready when the first of the guests started to arrive. When they had come home from work, they both had a short period of time to enjoy the last bit of peace and quiet together, before they went to join the party.

They knew all too soon their garden would be completely taken over, and maybe also their house.

They had seen the weather forecast earlier and it did not look too promising, with the chance of rain. If it did happen to rain, James and Sally had considered although there house was quite large, it would certainly be a squeeze if they had to accommodate all of the villagers inside. They both presumed in the event of bad weather the party would either finish early or maybe have to be postponed. The weather had been rather overcast as they came home from work, but as they were getting themselves ready for the party, the sky did clear and it did look after all as if the evenings weather was going to be fine.

Once they were ready for the party, they walked outside together, although it was still rather early they were both amazed to see their garden was now rather full and appeared to be very busy. The food had been carefully placed on the table. There was rather a vast array of food, bread, salad, cheese, cooked meat and of course a plentiful supply of buns and cakes. It was apparent that no one would go hungry. Sally struggled to find space on the table for her contribution.

James and Sally were both warmly greeted by everyone, with many thanks for allowing this village tradition to go ahead. There were a few faces here neither of them recognised, as well, of course, there were plenty of friends and acquaintances that they had made during the time they had lived in this village. They wandered around their garden chatting and mingling, everyone was just so friendly. As they were walking around, both James and Sally kept an eye out for Tony. They had not yet seen him, which seemed strange since he was the one who had persuaded them to host this party, they were surprised that he was not there at the start, and also he had not been there to do a lot of the organising and helping. They just had to presume he was there somewhere in the crowd and they both knew they would meet up with him before long.

The bar had been set up near the long food table. They wandered over towards the bar and managed to grab a drink, the bar area was pretty busy. James got out his wallet to pay for their drinks but this was brushed aside. Dave would not take any money for their drink. "We cannot thank you enough for allowing us to hold this party here again and to carry on with this tradition." James was beginning to wonder just what was so special about their garden, surely they could have broken this annual tradition just a little by holding the party somewhere else. There were certainly plenty of other gardens in this village that were large enough, or even the village green itself would have been suitable.

The noise level at the party was not too excessive, no one had been particularly loud, including the children, who had all been reasonably well behaved. There was certainly some noise though from the constant chatter of all these people. Without any warning though, the noise level seemed to decrease until there was almost silence. Sally found that she had stopped talking to a neighbour in mid-sentence to try to work out why there was this almost complete silence. Sally looked around at her friends and neighbours and realised that they were all looking upwards, gazing into the sky. Sally followed the stares and at first could not see anything other than a lovely blue sky. After a few seconds Sally did spot some movement in the sky some distance away, but could not make out what this was and why on earth everyone else was so fascinated? Sally looked over to where James was standing just a few feet away, he was also looking in awe just as were all the other guests, and also like Sally he was slightly puzzled.

The object in the sky, that was capturing all of the attention, appeared to be growing larger. This object, as it came closer, appeared to Sally to be just some kind of large bird, maybe a bird of prey or even a swan. James silently crept over to be closer to Sally, and without Sally realising he took hold of her hand, before they both knew what was actually happening they both felt this was a moment to share.

James suddenly became aware of what this object really was, but did not like to say a word to Sally, so he did not spoil the surprise for her. Instead they carried on silently gazing as the object came closer and closer.

Sally stood with James mesmerised, it began to slowly dawn on her what it was that had held their attention. This was not some large graceful bird at all, this was in fact their friend Tony, he was now looking somewhat different than Sally had ever seen him before, so much more graceful. Sally glanced up at James who whispered "this is not only our friend Tony, but it is also my guardian angel, Antonio." By this time, most of the villagers had gathered there, in James and Sally's garden. The garden was now almost full but Antonio managed to find one clear area on the lawn and landed there so gracefully.

James and Sally had been stood some distance away from where Antonio landed. They tried not to stare but they were both very curious to see Antonio the angel transform back into Tony the man. This transformation, although it seemed to happen relatively quickly, it was not a sudden movement, instead it seemed to happen rather gracefully. The wings just seem to disappear, neither of them had the chance to see where they went to. The wings Antonio had been flying with were very large, they were long and of course covered in feathers, but now there was no sign of them at all. Tony had produced a T shirt from somewhere and put this on in no time at all.

Almost as soon as he had landed, and had transformed from an angel to an ordinary looking man, Tony came striding over to James and Sally. They had been stood in amongst many of the other villagers, but Tony seemed to know exactly where they were. Perhaps Tony had spotted them from the air. James and Sally felt somewhat reserved. This was Tony, their good friend they had come to know so well, but they both felt as if they would like to congratulate him on this spectacular show they had both witnessed. Surely though this was not angel etiquette. James and Sally both though felt somewhat shy and instead commented on the great party.

"Many thanks to you both for allowing this party to go ahead," stated Tony. "It was not the same last year with the house being empty, it did not feel kind of right holding the party." "You still had the party here with the way the garden was, all over grown?" replied Sally remembering just what a sorry sight this garden had been when they had first moved in. "Couldn't you have held the party in another garden?" "No," replied Tony, quietly, "it had to be here. We did tidy the garden up a little first, but it wasn't the same, almost a bit like trespassing."

They did not have the opportunity to discuss this conversation further. There were several of the guests all trying to greet Tony at the same time. James and Sally took this chance to move away, and carried on mingling with other villagers.

Not long after Tony had arrived, Sally realised that Wendy and one or two others were uncovering the food in readiness for them all to eat. There was already a long queue of children waiting to eat. Sally wandered over to help and removed cling film and tin foil from plates and dishes of food. Sally handed out plates to some of the children and helped the younger ones with choosing their food.

Sally had expected all the adults to start queuing up once the children had been served. When she looked up though she saw that all the adults were still milling around chatting and no one had made any move to help themselves from the buffet. Wendy noticed that Sally looked a little surprised at this. "You will have to find James and get your food. No one else will take any food until the two of you have been served." Sally had to presume this was part of the tradition, or some unspoken politeness, that surrounded this party and off she went in search of James. Following Tony's quite spectacular arrival, Sally wondered if there were any more surprises to come or if this was it now. If there were to be no more surprises, then the party was certainly pleasant just as it was.

Sally soon found James not too far away from the food, talking to Christine and Bill. "Sorry to interrupt," said Sally looking at James, "but we need to go and eat." "Please do go and help yourself" replied Christine, with a smile, "then we can all go and get something to eat. I am getting a bit peckish." The food did look good and Sally realised that it had been a long time since lunch, she found now that she was now very hungry. Tony was hovering around as James and Sally approached the table and helped themselves to a plate. "Please be cautious with the food and try not to eat too much, as tempting as it all may seem." "Good heavens" replied James, "is there something wrong with the food, or are you worried about my waist line?" "Absolutely nothing wrong with the food," came the reply, "it would just be wise not to eat too much."

Sally decided maybe Tony was a little worried that there might not be enough food to go round, though there did seem to be plenty of it, maybe she had underestimated how many people there were here in their garden. As tempting as it all was, and despite such a huge choice they managed not to over fill their plates. They sat down on one of their own garden benches to eat. Nearly everyone else sat on chairs they had brought along with them or on blankets on the ground. The garden was full, but the atmosphere there was calm and peaceful considering, the number of villagers there. Both James and Sally had previously presumed their garden would be way over crowded with all these people in it, not to mention noisy, but surprisingly it was not too bad. There did seem to be plenty of space for everyone.

When Sally had finished eating, she wandered back over to the food and helped herself to a thin slice of cake, taking one for James as well. Sally could not help but notice that there was an abundance of food still left to eat, and by now everyone there at the party appeared to have been served. She shrugged and decided that Tony must have his reason, and managed to resist helping herself to seconds, although she certainly could have managed some more.

James and Sally spent the next hour or so, after they had finished eating, wandering around chatting to friends and neighbours. During this time they discovered that Christine and Bill were also keen walkers and they arranged to go out walking with them the following weekend. Christine and Bill promised to show them different walks around the area, places that James and Sally had yet to explore. They also received several other invitations from villagers, people who previously they had only smiled at in passing. These offers included several vague invitations for them to pop in for a cup of coffee, or an evening drink and a more solid invitation for them to attend a dinner party the weekend after next, their social life suddenly seemed a lot busier.

As they were wandering around they passed by the food table. Sally could not help but notice the ample supply of leftover food was now once again covered over. She just hoped that this food would not go to waste. The food would probably be uncovered again later, so that a few of them could have seconds.

"Hi" greeted Tony, strolling over to James and Sally. "Please could I ask you one more favour this evening?" "No problem" replied James looking slightly puzzled. "Could we please have the use of your outbuilding?" requested Tony, nodding over towards the old shed. Even more curious thought James, but he could not refuse.

James had automatically locked their house as they came outside to the party, he did not know why at the time he had done so since they were going to spend the evening in their own garden. Since he had locked the house though, this did mean that James also had the key to the outbuilding with him. James, Sally and Tony walked slowly over to this old building. James unlocked it when they got there, but then he stood back to allow Tony to enter first.

When James had unlocked the door and turned round to let Tony go past he noticed that the three of them were not alone. Many of the villagers had followed them, there was quite a crowd waiting outside the building, this building which was really not much more than just a dilapidated old shed, James and Sally were both by now somewhat alarmed as they knew there was no way the whole of the village was going to fit inside this shed. It was not as if there was any need for shelter as the evening was still plenty warm enough without a hint of rain.

Tony noticed their concern and smiled, "Don't worry, we won't disturb anything in here. This is another part of this old tradition." Tony strode over to the far end of the outbuilding, to the door James had occasionally ventured through, and had presumed that he was the only one who knew about. Tony of course knew about this door as without any hesitation he bent down to the moon and star and soon had the door leading to the year 1905 opened. He held the door open and gestured for James and Sally to pass through. This time, to Tony's relief, Sally could not bring herself to refuse. James could feel her tense up slightly at the side of him and knew she would be feeling somewhat apprehensive. James took Sally's hand and together they walked through the door, and into the past.

On passing through into this strange world they both gave a small gasp. There were fields here, as James had seen before. These fields though could have been anywhere, and not necessarily the fields of their own village one hundred

127

years in the past. What really did surprise them both though was the footpath, James had never seen this footpath when he had ventured here previously. The way forward from the door was laid out for them in flagstones, each one having the crescent moon and star on, this very unique design they were both now becoming very familiar with.

James and Sally had paused for only a moment or two on the threshold of the two worlds, they both turned to glance at Tony, they needed him to give his permission for them to enter on to the footpath. They realised there was now a large crowd of villagers waiting expectantly, but patiently behind Tony. "Please lead the way," requested Tony. "Tonight you are both the guests of honour."

Guests of honour at what James and Sally did not know, however they were both very curious to know, and felt obliged to continue on their way along the footpath. "This is how Dorothy must have felt as she made her way along the yellow brick road," said Sally, with a smile. They both felt as if their adventure this evening was just beginning. Sally had not previously wanted to venture into the past, but now, with the whole of the village following them, surely it was safe to do so, there was no way she could now refuse.

James and Sally walked along the path hand in hand, at the side of them was Tony. They did not have to walk too far when they saw up ahead of them what surely must be their destination. In front of them they could see a bonfire, with another large crowd gathered around it. James and Sally slowed down and approached this crowd tentatively. They might both have been tempted to turn round and flee for home if Tony had not been beside them, not to mention the mass of their own villagers, who were right behind them. As they approached this gathering of people, everyone in the crowd turned around to face them, very soon James and Sally could see many warm smiling faces looking at them.

The first person Tony introduced them to was the farmer, Ted, the one James had found himself working for and the one that he had since had a pint with. James knew he would never again be intimidated by this farmer, he really was kind and very friendly. All around James and Sally, people were shaking hands and hugging. There were so many people here, all being greeted like long lost friends, which they obviously must be, if they only got to meet up with each other once a year on this one very special evening.

The site of this party was not in the same area as James and Sally's garden, they had only walked a relatively short distance from their own garden. They were now though in a large field, which James realised, must be about in the same place Pete and Wendy's farm was situated.

They were then introduced to the farmer's wife, Sadie, she was very jolly and friendly, but also at the same time looked slightly harassed. Sally stood awhile talking to Sadie and was somewhat surprised to hear that she too had five children which also included a set of twins. Sally then noticed all of these ten children, from both sets of farmers had all met up and were now playing together as if they had in fact known each other for ever, rather than their meeting on this one evening a year.

Now she was actually here at this strange party, Sally no longer did feel at all scared. She had been very wary when she realised that she had to go through the back door of the old shed, but now she was here Sally was very much enjoying the atmosphere.

Sadie had moved off and Sally was left alone for a moment or two. Whilst Sally was stood there she could smell something rather delicious. Looking around she was amazed to see a whole pig roasting not too far from where she stood. Was this the reason Tony had told them not to eat too much, that they were now going to be fed again? This was also probably the reason why Sadie was looking slightly harassed, it was clearly her responsibility to organise the food at this party. James had been stood not too far from Sally talking to farmer Ted. He came to join Sally. "Having a good time?" James asked, "I wouldn't have missed this for anything, it is truly amazing."

James and Sally wandered around together for a while. They were being constantly stopped. Many of the villagers of one hundred years ago came over to introduce themselves. All of the villagers of the old Marton cum Tiddleworth made James and Sally very welcome. These villagers all seemed to know who they were, that they were the new owners of the house on Whisper Lane, the house where access could be gained between the two worlds. Sally was certainly made to feel very special, as if the two of them were indeed the guests of honour.

While they were wandering around and chatting to old and new friends and neighbours the sky in the distance seemed to be darkening. The dark cloud was too far away to hopefully spoil this party, but still it was rather dark and it appeared to be raining some distance away. Here though at the party it was still warm enough not to worry too much.

James and Sally came across Tony again, there were so many questions to ask him, but realised they were not going to get the chance now and probably not at all this evening. As they were stood there both of Wendy's twins came up and asked excitedly, "Uncle Tony, is there going to be a rainbow?" "I wouldn't be at all surprised," replied Tony, "and you two can have the first slide." "What sort of rainbow is it that you can slide down?" Sally was curious to know. "Come with us, we can all go and search for a rainbow together." With this Tony set off at quite a pace across the field in the direction of the dark rain clouds. They had only got half way across the field when one of the twins started jumping up and down. "I can see the rainbow, there it is." Sally looked to where one of the children was pointing, it was not a very bright rainbow, but a rainbow it certainly was.

James, Sally, Tony and the twins went a little bit further across the field and as they got closer the rainbow certainly was getting brighter and one end of it did seem to touch down to the ground, only about fifty yards away. Sally knew though of course it was not possible for the rainbow to be on the ground, that what they were seeing was just an illusion.

Once again though Sally was proved to be wrong. This rainbow really did come down to the ground. Tony and the twins had gathered speed and before she realised Tony was lifting one twin up on to the rainbow and allowed her to slide down it. "Me next," shouted her sister excitedly. Sally and James stood and watched amazed for a few minutes while the twins took turns to slide down the rainbow. The rainbow did appear to be very solid, with all of the colours standing out. Sally could not resist, and wandered over to see what a rainbow felt like to touch. The rainbow looked almost solid, each of these colours of the rainbow looked very vibrant and did stand out very clearly. Both James and Sally went to put their hands on the rainbow, but there was nothing there, they seemed to be feeling just air, nothing solid. Sally looked across at Tony, but he just shrugged and smiled as if he also did not have an answer for this phenomenon.

While James and Sally were puzzling over this amazing rainbow, they realised there were many more children, from both centuries, clamouring to have a turn. It looked as if Tony could be busy all night. "Do you know how long the rainbow will last, or is it permanent?" Sally wanted to know. "No, it is not permanent, but it should at least last long enough for all of the young ones to have a go." James and Sally stayed there for some time watching all the children have a go. There was no pushing or shoving, they all seemed to be happy to wait their turn, and then they joined the back of the queue again, to see if there was a chance for another go. It was as if they all knew that the rainbow would be there at least long enough for them all to have at least one turn each, and maybe if they were lucky, another one.

After, maybe thirty minutes or so, the rainbow started to fade. Then when one of the older children was having a go, he got almost to the bottom of the slide, when he suddenly fell through the rainbow and landed on the ground with a bump. He got up and started laughing, he was certainly not in the least bit injured. "I guess," said Tony, "that it must be time to go and eat. Is anyone hungry?" "No," protested several of the children, "it is not time to eat yet, what about the rainbow blob."

"No rainbow blob, not this year," replied Tony with a smile. "Yes there it is," clamoured the rather excited children. Sally was not that unduly surprised over what was another strange encounter. The rainbow had faded from the sky but the remnants of the rainbow were still clearly visible on the ground, just yards from where they were standing. It did appear to be one large blob of colour. All of the colours of the rainbow stood out and then merged into each other at the bottom, just where it almost touched the ground. The colours were all still there but rather than an arch going up into the sky, this was just a mass of colours hovering just over the ground.

This rainbow blob did not appear to be too large, but all the children, at least twenty or thirty of them rushed into the mass of colours. James and Sally hung back, not so sure if this experience was something only for the children, but with encouragement from Tony they also entered the rainbow blob. "Wow," said Sally in amazement, "this is quite something." Inside the rainbow blob it was just like stepping into a Tardis, it was not huge, but certainly bigger than it appeared to be from the outside. They were bombarded with all the colours of the rainbow, these colours were much more intense from the inside than they had appeared to be on the outside, so much more vivid. The colours were not static but swirled about, intertwining with each other.

"Wow this is amazing, it is like being inside some amazing light show." This was not only an experience with light, but there was another vivid experience that made both Sally and James jump at first. They could feel a rather pleasant tingling feeling all over their skin, something like being bathed in a bath full of a fizzy sherbet. Each colour had its own different sensation. There was a soothing mellow sensation from the red and yellow, but the purple colour was stronger, as if their skin were being struck by hundreds of tiny little pins.

While James, Sally and Tony were stood in this rainbow blob the children were darting about, chasing around, trying to capture the colours. A part of Sally also wanted to rush around like the children, but she did just stand there with James and Tony amazed by this wonderful experience. She could not resist holding out her arms so that she could really feel the sensation on her skin.

James and Sally had been stood there entranced for maybe ten or fifteen minutes when the rainbow blob started to fade. It seemed to become very gradually smaller, the colours faded and the tingly sensation on the skin also faded. A few moments more and they were stood outside in the cool night air, the rainbow blob had now vanished completely. Sally shivered a little, the night air suddenly felt somewhat cooler. "Now," said Tony, "it really is time to eat, is anyone hungry?"

Once again James and Sally found they had to lead the queue for another buffet. They were both surprised to find that in the hour or so that had passed since the first buffet they were both once again reasonably hungry. For this meal they were given thick slices of bread and pork, with beer to wash the food down with. It all tasted really delicious.

James and Sally sat on benches at a long table. It was all rather basic but there was such a great atmosphere. Although the temperature had dropped, the weather remained about warm enough so they could sit outside without feeling too cold.

There was not enough room for everyone to sit at these benches, so the children were sat around in groups on the grass. Sally was surprised to realise that although she should not have been unduly hungry, she had no problem at all in tucking into this second meal. She felt very greedy.

James and Sally found themselves sitting close to their neighbours Christine and Bill. Christine introduced them to another couple from the old village. This couple also happened to be called Christine and Bill. Sally did vaguely wonder if there could be another couple here called James and Sally. This couple were a youngish married couple. Christine ran the small village school, the same school that had closed down many years ago, prior to James and Sally moving to the village. Bill of one hundred years ago worked a few miles away at a grammar school.

Sally was keen to hear about the old village school, how many children attended, what the lessons were like and also about the school discipline. Sally could have sat there all night talking to this Christine. "I tell you what, if you like on some other day, you are more than welcome to visit the school and see it all for yourself. Tonight of course there isn't the time and it has now all been locked up" "Wow that would be great," replied Sally, "I love the idea of these small village schools, and it would be great to see what resources you use."

They sat together talking for some time after the meal, when Sally realised that several ladies had got up and had started to clear the tables. Sally also then jumped up to help but was quickly made to sit back down again. "Maybe next year you can help us, but tonight just enjoy the party." Sally felt a bit guilty but obliged and sat down and turned once more to Christine to ask more questions about school life, such as what the children wrote on, and what with, and what time they started and finished their school day.

After the tables had been cleared a group of musicians gathered up their instruments and started to play. It was not long before young and old folk alike got up to dance. Sally would have been quite content to sit and enjoy the very lively music and watch the dancers, but she was not allowed to do this. Tony came over and dragged her up. Sally had never danced to any folk music before, but Tony was an excellent dancer and Sally had no problem at all in following his lead. At the end of the first dance there was a short pause and Sally saw not too far away, that James was also dancing. He had been dragged up to dance, by Sadie.

Sally was slightly out of breath after the first dance and was all ready to go and find a seat, but she did not have the chance. "You don't get away that easily," said Ted "it is my turn now for this next dance." It was some time later before Sally did get to sit down again and have a well-earned rest and a drink to quench her thirst. She seemed to have lost James, not that it mattered, she had plenty of company. Sally only managed to sit out one dance before she found herself being claimed again for another dance.

Over the course of the evening Sally had many dances, each time with a different partner, for only one of the dances she was able to partner James, though together they struggled somewhat to keep up with everyone else. Sally was soon able to keep up with the dances and was surprised to find she was able to do so without treading on anyone's feet.

Sally found she was really enjoying this incredible experience, but before long Sally realised that the band was announcing the last dance of the night. Once again Tony came over and insisted upon this dance. It was all very lively, Sally managed to keep up but was feeling tired at the end. It had certainly been a long day. When the music came to an end Tony announced they would have to find James, it was now late and time to head home.

James was not far away, he had had the last dance with Sadie. Sally looked slightly saddened as she informed James that it was time for them all to leave. "Will we be able to come back again sometime?" James asked of Tony looking somewhat deflated. "We will definitely be back this time next year, if we can use your outbuilding again?"

Looking around them James and Sally could see many more sad faces not to mention quite a few tears. Tony, along with James and Sally led the way back along the path on the route which would return them to their own world. Everyone behind them was quiet now and much more subdued. They were all saddened by the end of the party and having to say goodbye to so many old friends. No one particularly seemed it, but it was also more than likely that everyone must be really tired, particularly the younger children. They had all now been partying for several hours.

As they got to the part of the path where they had to re-enter their own world Tony stopped and looked up and indicated the now very dark sky, well almost dark. The sky now was just amazing. So amazing that James and Sally came to an abrupt stop causing two or three children who had been following them to suddenly run into the back of them.

"Wow" was all that James could come up with, the whole village was now transfixed by the amazing light show that was taking place in the night sky. It had been a full moon, and a very starry night, but now the sky had changed. There were shafts of light coming downwards from the dark night sky. These shafts of light were a wonderful assortment of colours, purple, green, blue, turquoise, not to mention many others. Neither James, nor Sally had ever been fortunate enough to witness the Northern lights, but this experience tonight must be very similar. Sally could not decide if this was the Northern lights, that had somehow become visible in their sky, or maybe, was it just possible the rainbow, from earlier, had returned and was now visible at night. Either explanation would normally seemed impossible. She was certainly far too absorbed in watching this phenomenon to ask.

Sally took her eyes off this amazing light show for a few seconds to glance around at the other villagers. They were all gazing up at this awesome sight, there was complete silence from everyone. They must have all been stood there for some time, maybe fifteen or twenty minutes before the colours started to slowly fade and the sky returned to an intense black, with light coming from thousands of stars and also of course the moon.

Everyone seemed even more subdued once the light show had finished. James and Sally in particular were reluctant to move away in case they missed anything else. The pair of them had both experienced such a lot this evening, but this light show had really been the icing on the cake. "It is time to leave this world behind." Tony had to urge them on the last part of the journey. With no problem Tony opened the door back into their own world and all the villagers from 2005 returned back into James and Sally's garden. The party really was now over.

Leftover food, chairs and blankets were quietly and efficiently gathered up and with a few quiet thank you's and farewells to James and Sally, everyone left, back to their own lives and for the majority to bed. It now really was very late.

When everyone had gone, Sally looked around their garden. Even though it was very dark, Sally was able to see it had now almost been cleared of all of the party debris. All of the mess and rubbish had been removed and it was now hard to imagine that a party had taken place here only a few short hours ago.

Tony was the last person to leave and before he did he came to say goodbye. "Can I please thank you both for allowing our midsummers eve party to take place." "We would not have missed this evening for anything, it has all been so amazing," replied James. Tony went on to explain that with their permission this party would continue to be an annual occasion, and would continue as long as James and Sally were living at this cottage. "We can never be certain if this event could be possible with different owners of this property. It only seems to be with the right people living here that we are able to access into the village of one hundred years ago."

Tony explained that although the whole village looked forward to this event every year, in fact there was very little talk of it. "Even the youngest of the children seem to know not to talk of the party outside of this village."

"When we spent all that time looking at houses, we had not at all considered moving to this village, and our plans had not included buying an older property that needed so much renovating. Do you think it was possible this house was looking for us, rather than the other way around?" Sally wanted to know. "Whoever knows," replied Tony, though he seemed to have a smile around his eyes as if he really did know this answer.

CHAPTER ELEVEN

Understandably it took James and Sally some time that night to fall asleep. They both lay in bed for a good hour or so remembering and discussing every last little detail of their amazing evening. They knew though they had to be at work the following day as they continued talking into the early hours of the morning, but it was so hard to get to sleep after all the excitement.

They did of course both eventually get to sleep and were not too surprised to find they had slept a bit later than usual. They sat for a short while and had a rather hurried breakfast together. Naturally enough the only conversation they shared that morning, before they had to dash off to work was on the Mid summers eve parties.

After a busy day at work, once again, over their evening meal, the conversation was all about both of the parties. James asked the question. "Now you have been once, how would you now feel about having another walk through our village of one hundred years ago?" Sally was thoughtful at this question, however she was not instantly dismissive as she would have been previously. Sally sat and thought about the idea for a few minutes. "Mmm, I would very much like to see what the village itself looked like all those years ago. We didn't get to see too much of it last night. It would also be interesting to meet up with friends again, the ones we made last night."

"I must admit," replied James, "it would be great to go and have another beer at the Duck and Cow, the beer did taste different, it seemed to somehow have a more intense flavour. I have no idea though how I would pay for a pint in the old pub, maybe Tony will know the answer to this problem."

When they eventually finished their meal, Sally cleared away the dishes while James went to make a coffee. There was an unexpected knock at the door, it was Tony, who else! He seemed to have a knack of calling when they were both at home and not too busy. Tony joined them as they sat and had another coffee. James and Sally were able to put a few unanswered questions to him, particularly the one James was keen to know, about buying a pint in the old Duck and Cow. "You will find if you were to help out on the farm every now and again, you will automatically earn a free drink in the pub. "Wow that does seem like a good bargain," replied James, "providing it is mainly help in the fields rather than with the animals."

There were so many questions both of them wanted to know about the time travelling, one in particular Sally asked of Tony, "Is it possible for me to bake a cake or biscuits to take there and share them?" "No," replied Tony, "It is not possible to take food. We have tried before, although the plates and tins remain intact, for some reason the food seems to perishes and turns into dust as soon as we cross the time gap. This is why we have to do the party the way we do. If we all eat something before we go then we are not going across there too hungry and eat up all of their food. They are always very generous, but we have always to presume they may not have too much food to spare."

"Can the time travel work in the opposite direction, could the party be held in this garden in the present year?" James wanted to enquire. "No" Tony replied, "Again time travel has been tried on a hand full of occasions by some of the adults from one hundred years ago. They have stepped over the line into this world and very suddenly they have felt unwell. They have complained of palpitations and shivering, I have witnessed this happening. Farmer Ted tried to come over here not that long ago, he was curious about our life. I have never seen anyone looking so grey and haggard before.

Fortunately though, when anyone has stepped over here across the time gap to 2005, than as soon as they return back to their own world in 1905, their health does immediately restore. Oddly enough, I don't know if you have noticed, but the opposite seems to work for us over here. Everyone always looks so well after this party. Many of the villagers have commented that their minor ailments such as headaches or coughs and colds seem to vanish on the night of the party. We cannot be sure if there really is any magic quality in the air over there, or if it is just a case of everyone having such a good time at the party they forget about all their aches and pains."

Two or three weeks went by uneventfully. James and Sally were kept busy with their own lives, though the thought of adventuring back into the old village was never far away. They did manage to escape across there one Saturday afternoon. This time Sally was equally as keen to go as James was, she no longer needed any persuading.

Once they had crossed over the time gap, they wandered in the direction of the farm, the same farm where James had helped out and where the party had been held. They came upon Farmer Ted who was once more busy, this time ploughing a field. He looked up and spotted them walking in his direction. "Do you need a hand?" asked James. "That would be great, if you have nothing better to do with your time." James looked towards Sally and asked if it would be OK, if he could help on the farm for about half an hour. "Mmm, that's fine with me, I may just wander over to have a word with Sadie, do you want to come over and meet me there when you have finished helping here?" "Will Sadie mind if I pop and see her?" Sally asked of Ted. "I am sure that she will be glad of the company," replied Ted.

Sadie was only too pleased to see Sally again, and before very long Sally found herself helping out with the children, mainly keeping all of them amused while Sadie was able to get on with a few household chores. The time passed very quickly and Sally soon realised she had been there for an hour or more. James came to find her and was quite apologetic for being late. Sally had to admit it had not occurred to her that he was late.

"Ted is just going for a drink to the pub, do you mind very much if I go along as well?" "No problem" said Sally, "I also wouldn't mind a drink, I will come along as well." James looked a bit sheepish, "I am really sorry but you can't come with us, it is not really the done thing here." Sadie had been listening to this conversation and had been a little taken back by it, that Sally had suggested going to the pub. Sally realised her mistake, it was not really the most appropriate thing here for her to go to the pub. Sally did remember though that Christine had promised her that when she was in this village again she would be more than happy for her to visit.

"You go to the pub with Ted" replied Sally "I will go and visit Christine. If she is not around or if she is busy, I will be more than happy to have a wander round the village. I will meet you by the duck pond in about an hour." "Ok," said James, "I will try not to be late this time." They left the farmhouse together, with James and Ted stopping off at the Duck and Cow and Sally walking a little bit further, stopping at the house next door to the village school.

Christine answered the door to Sally's knock and was delighted to see her and was very pleased for the chance to show off the village school. The school was really only very small. It was a single storey building with one relatively large classroom. The school, Sally found out, took between twenty to thirty children. All of the children, aged five up to eleven, were taught here in this one classroom. Sally could not imagine what it would be like teaching several different subjects at the same time to such a wide age range, it must pose some challenges.

Sally was very much entranced with the school and it was more than obvious that Christine was very proud of it. Sally thought about all the technology that was available to her at the school she taught at. Sally would have loved to have been able to help Christine out with some more modern equipment and resources, she knew though this was not possible. Sally thought about talking to Tony about this, but she knew what the answer would be, taking any equipment over here would not be possible.

After a tour of the school Sally returned with Christine to her house where they had a chat over a cup of tea, they spoke mainly about school subjects and discipline. Sally found out that Christine also had the same problems with discipline that she often experienced. They were able to swap stories and suggestions on ways to tackle the problem.

The hour quickly passed, before too long Sally realised that she would have to go and look for James. "Many thanks for showing me around and for the tea, would it be possible for me to come and visit again sometime?" "Of course you can, I would enjoy another chat about school life." replied Christine, as she went with Sally to the door to wave her off.

Sally walked the short distance over to the duck pond and sat down on the grass to wait for James to come out of the pub. It was a pleasant day, there were several children playing by the pond. Sally was sitting comfortably on the grass, and was enjoying the scene in front of her when not only James and farmer Ted, but also Tony, came out of the pub.

The three of them joined Sally on the grass for just a few minutes before Ted got up to go. "Someone has to go and milk the cows, I don't suppose any of you want to come and help?" James face seemed to drain of colour, but Tony got up straight away and offered to help. Tony turned to James and Sally and asked if they could find their own way home. "No problem" replied James, all too quickly, he now seemed in a great hurry to get back home. "Actually" replied Sally, "I would love to learn how to milk a cow. I have never before had the opportunity to milk a cow, but I would like to have a go?" Tony and farmer Ted looked at Sally, slightly surprised, they had presumed James reluctance to perform this task would also extend to Sally, "but "why not, Sadie will be there, she will be able to show you what to do."

Reluctantly James followed them. Amazingly Sally had no problem with milking the cows, she soon picked up the knack of what to do. Sally found it really satisfying, seeing the bucket fill with the warm, creamy milk. James had hung back when they arrived at the barn, but now seeing Sally manage with the milking so easily, then he also reluctantly had a go. He was not as adept as Sally, but he was relieved to find he was not totally useless at this, and at least none of the cows kicked him, or even knocked over the bucket of milk.

James and Sally went home soon after the milking session was over, along with Tony. Tony was more than happy to take on Sally's offer of sharing their evening meal. That morning, before they set out on their adventure Sally had made a lasagne and knew there would be more than enough for the three of them to share. While the lasagne was cooking slowly in the oven Sally prepared a salad to go with it and she also laid out the table.

James and Tony were a little relieved when Sally turned down their offer of help and they made themselves quite comfortable in the living room with another beer apiece. Sally was actually pleased to be by herself for a short while so she could remember her pleasant afternoon, and relive the experience. She could not decide which part of the afternoon she had enjoyed the most, the time spent with Sadie and all her children, the time spent with Christine and the old school room or milking the cows. It was great to think she would be able to go over there again in the not too distant future.

As they were eating their meal, Sally could not help bring up the subject of the old Marton cum Tiddleworth. "This amazing chance we have of living here and being able to visit our village as it was one hundred years ago is really something very special, but is there anything more we can do to help with their lives?"

Tony took a deep breath before going on to explain this was not possible. "We have tried previously taking some of

149

our farming equipment into the old village, but it just does not work. We cannot obviously take anything too large, but we have tried to take spades and other small pieces of equipment. We have found though when we get them over there, they do seem very quickly to rust and start to decay. If we were to take equipment over there regularly, even just for a short while, it would be very costly, and quite impractical. Any damage that does occur to the equipment over there, does not restore itself if we return it to the present day.

I should already have warned you also, you should not wear any decent clothing when you venture over there. We have noticed again clothing is susceptible to changes, fortunately nothing embarrassing has occurred but clothing does seem to somehow age over there, it is best to stick to old jeans and a T shirt, clothing that is quite tough, and you are not too bothered about if it is spoiled."

"When I think of all the resources and technology we have access to in this present day, it does seem a shame though we cannot share some of it." "It cannot be done though," replied Tony. "Even if we could take anything with us that would not be susceptible to damage, we still could not do this without the chance of changing the course of history, even if this is in a very small way. Marton cum Tiddleworth of one hundred years ago has to be enjoyed and respected just as it is, we have to leave it as it is and do our best not to change it."

"Besides, you seem to have enjoyed doing the milking while we were there this afternoon," this was directed at Sally, while James gave a small grimace, "it would not be the same as helping to milk cows on a present day farm. Just imagine the machines that are used today. You will probably not be so keen to help Pete milk his cows. We do sometimes get into a discussion over there about the way life is here, but I often get the impression that those villagers are not always that interested, and do not always seem to believe us. It is not very easy explaining the concept of computers and mobile phones."

Sally had to agree with this and knew deep down Tony was right, they would not want do anything that could in any way change the course of history. "Could we though, go and visit the old Marton cum Tiddleworth whenever we like?" James was keen to know. "Mmm, within reason," replied Tony. The more frequently you visit, then the more likely it is you actually are of changing the course of history, even in a small way, Certainly the more often you go across the time gap then there is a greater chance of our time travel being discovered by someone from outside this village. The rest of the villagers from 2005 only visit the old village just once a year, on mid summers eve.

It would not make too much of a difference though if the pair of you were to spend the odd weekend afternoon over there as you did today. You can still go and have a chat and help out in a small way. You will have to bear in mind though, it is possible while you are over there, a friend or relative from outside this village could be trying to contact you. It would be hard to explain a prolonged absence, it was a bit easier in the days before mobile phones came on the scene. It is now harder to say that you had been out somewhere and had both forgotten to take your phones with you!"

"It would be great to keep in touch with the friends we have made over there, on a more regular basis rather than for only the yearly party. We will try to limit our visits to maybe just once a month at the most."

"I presume mobile phones don't work over there?" Sally was curious to know. She asked with a bit of a grin as she was certain what the answer would be. "You are right," replied Tony. "They don't work and I would suggest you do not even try taking one, time travel does seem to have a strange effect on them. I took mine over there not so long ago, I had not meant to do so, and went and left it switched on. When I returned the clock on it would only go backwards. I did take it in for repair but they could not mend it. They did want to know what on earth I had done with it. Surprisingly though I can fortunately still use it as a phone. You do have to be careful with what you do take over there."

After this day James and Sally did their best to restrict their visits to about once a month, and also they were careful not to go exactly once a month, on the same day, just in case close family or friends became curious. Sally's mum, in particular did phone her frequently, usually on a weekend. Sally could not come up with too many reasons as to where they were, and did not feel particularly comfortable lying to her mum.

Sometimes they went across to the old village on a Saturday and sometimes they went on a Sunday. Occasionally they also went on a week day if they happened to both be on holiday at the same time. They did their best to ensure that it was unlikely no one would ring or call in. They now always planned these trips together. Every time that they went it was always something of a treat, something to look forward to and of course it gave them both plenty to talk about. Several times they made a prior arrangement with Tony and would walk through to the other side with him. There were also occasions when they hadn't made a prior arrangement, but bumped into Tony over there anyway.

When they visited the old village James was always happy to spend time working on the farm, preferably in the fields, harvesting or planting out new crops. James own job, as an accountant, meant sitting behind a desk for long periods, it was good for him to get out into the fresh air and to do some manual labour. He knew he could have spent the time working in his own garden, but somehow over here it seemed less of a chore. He was still not so keen though to work with the farm animals.

Sally however was happy to work with the animals, she was frequently to be found either collecting the eggs or milking the cows. After a couple of hours work James then very much enjoyed a pint in the Duck and Cow. He was beginning to get to know these villagers over here very well, almost as well as the ones in the present day pub. James often felt quite guilty because Sally was not able to join him in this pub. Sally though was never too bothered, only slightly curious. Instead Sally was more than happy to go and have a chat with Christine and to discuss the way a junior school was run in this period of time. She was keen to learn about the school curriculum and also the discipline. Sally realised that she was gaining good knowledge about this period that could be useful for the history lessons in her school, but she would have to be careful in that she did not give away too much information.

CHAPTER TWELVE

Several months after the midsummer party James found one weekend afternoon when he went over to the old village by himself. James and Sally had originally planned to go together and James had kind of promised to help Ted in the fields. Sally though did not feel up to going. James was somewhat concerned, as well as a bit surprised as these days Sally was as keen as he was on their trips to the old village. "I do not have to go, I can always stay here with you and we can go together next weekend." "No it's OK" said Sally. "I just feel a bit off it, nothing to worry about. I have probably caught something from one of the children at school. I would certainly not like to take any germs over there. I shall stay here at home and curl up with a book."

Sally did have her suspicion about what really was causing her tiredness, it certainly wasn't something that she had picked up at school, but she was reluctant to find out just yet in case her hopes were dashed, maybe another week or so and she would find out for definite. Sally wasn't really feeling too unwell, she should have been able to go with James if he had been going anywhere else, but she had no idea at all about the effects time travel could possibly have on the early stages of pregnancy, if her instincts did turn out to be correct. She certainly didn't want to take any risks.

Sally sat and pondered for a while over this problem. She did not wish to excite James yet as to what she believed was reason for her tiredness, she certainly did not want to let anyone else know her secret before she chose to share it with James, he had to be the first to know. Maybe in a couple of weeks the best person to consult with would be Wendy, it was more than likely that she would have time travelled when pregnant, at least one of her pregnancies must have occurred over midsummer.

Once James had left, Sally sat down in a comfy armchair and curled up with her book. She was half reading the book but was finding it difficult to concentrate. It was the first time she had had to herself over the last week or so, and now Sally found that she was by herself, she was lost in her thoughts thinking about her possible lovely news.

As Sally had been sat there for a while she became vaguely aware of a gentle noise somewhere in the background. Sally had left a window open in the dining room and she could hear this sound coming through the window, even though she was in another room. It was not a particular warm day, but it felt pleasant to have some fresh air circulating through the house.

Sally put down her book. This sound, although it was not loud, was persistent and was becoming rather distracting. The noise sounded like that of a wind whistling through trees, today though the weather was too calm for this noise. Sally tried to ignore the sound and went back to her book, she had got very comfy, the book was good and she was reluctant to be disturbed. Sally read a few more paragraphs but realised that she was not going to be left in peace. The sound of the wind whistling through the trees was certainly continuing and if anything it was getting a little louder, it was becoming more obvious.

Eventually Sally gave a big sigh and put down the book once more. For one reason or another, it was obvious she was not going to be able to concentrate on it. Sally looked out through the window, she could see several trees, but they were barely moving. The whistling noise continued. Sally was now beginning to wonder if there was a problem somewhere in or around the house. She opened the back door and stepped outside. Out here the noise was definitely more apparent. There was nothing particularly loud or threatening about the sound but it was rather strange.

Sally was becoming concerned and felt as if she did have a small dilemma. She obviously could not talk about this noise to James as he was not there, and she could not contact him on his mobile, but there was no one else around. The closest neighbours, Christine and Bill, would probably help but it seemed such a strange trivial thing to go and seek help about, they would just think she was being a bit paranoid. This noise though did seem very persistent. Sally knew that she could not settle down again with her book until she had discovered the source of this sound. Sally suddenly realised of course there was one person she could ask for help, Tony. He would probably not think her strange, she just hoped that Tony was around.

Without further hesitation Sally picked up the phone and luckily Tony was at home, he answered almost immediately. Sally quickly explained the reason for the phone call, and apologised for it sounding trivial, she still half expected Tony not to take her seriously. Sally was therefore somewhat taken aback when Tony stated "Stay right there, I am coming over," and he immediately hung up.

Sally stared at the phone in amazement, it was only a noise from the trees around the house, certainly no emergency. Sally had barely time to replace the phone and walk over to the window to look out for Tony when he was there. Sally had no idea how he got there so quickly. When Tony arrived he did seem to have a concerned look on his face. "We have to go over to the other side, this only happens when there is a problem over there, usually a problem for someone who is from this period in time. I presume that James has gone over to help on the farm?"

Sally hesitated, any other time she would have gone over there straight away, particularly now that Tony had implied that James could be in danger. Tony saw the look of uncertainty that Sally had, "don't worry about the baby, it will be quite safe. Wendy went across several times when she was expecting." "But how on earth did you know?" "Oh, don't worry, your secret is safe with me. I shan't tell a soul, not even James, congratulations by the way, but we really must be off."

Without further ado Tony made his way to the outbuilding which fortunately was still unlocked from earlier, when James had set off. Tony quickly unlocked the entrance to the secret world and set off at speed towards the farm. Sally had difficulty keeping up with him, she was rather surprised that Tony obviously knew exactly where he was going and Sally of course was now very anxious about James.

They very quickly came to a field on the edge of the farm and saw a small commotion there. Sally's worst fears were confirmed, it was James who had had an accident. He had managed to get in the way of a sickle and had sustained quite a deep gash on his right leg. Sally looked on in horror and found herself having a problem with knowing what to do to help. Sally had done some first aid training, she had to do because of her job, but this was different, it was hard to be level headed about it when the accident had happened to someone so close. Tony though immediately took charge. He pulled a piece of clean white cloth out from somewhere, presumably a pocket, and wrapped this around the wound and applied some firm but gentle pressure, trying not to cause any more discomfort than was actually necessary.

The pressure to the wound seemed to stem the flow of blood, but it still obviously needed urgent medical attention. The wound would require stitching and James was obviously in pain. Sally was knelt at James side, she was clearly upset over the injury. Tony though remained calm and knew what had to be done. Sally was aware they had to get James to

159

casualty but the nearest emergency hospital was not only about seven miles away, but also a hundred years away. James would not be able to walk on his leg until it had been attended to and there was no way that Sally could bring the car right here.

Tony seemed to have read her mind. "I can take James back to your house, but will you be able to find your own way back?" Sally had never crossed the border by herself before, she had also never unlocked the door to this world but had seen it being done often enough. "No problem," replied Sally, "I will meet you back at the house and then take James to casualty in the car."

Tony stood up, he had been kneeling down next to James. He gave a big stretch and his back seemed to broaden and slowly his wings unfurled. Farmer Ted was there with one or two of the farm hands, and between them they carefully helped James up and on to Tony's back. Sally knew she had to return back to her house, she did not have time to waste, but could not help but pause to watch this awesome, rather beautiful sight.

Sally was naturally very concerned about James injury, the gash did look rather deep. She was also worried about how safe he would be on Antonio's back, and also worried that Antonio would not be able to fly safely with the extra weight that he was carrying. There was also a small part of Sally that was a little bit jealous, she could not help wonder if one day she might have the opportunity to fly on the wings of an angel.

She could not consider this for long though, she had to hurry off back to the house. Sally was pleased when Ted, without asking, came with her, at least as far as the wall, the part of the wall where she was able to gain access back into her own world. As they reached this part of the wall Ted bent down and pressed on the moon and star brick causing the entrance to give way and allowing Sally to pass through.

Here they had to say a quick goodbye. "I do hope that leg is soon mended. I am sorry I am not able to come any further with you." With this last remark Ted turned round and returned to his land. Sally quickly hurried to the front of her house and dashed inside for the car keys. She came out of the house just as Antonio was landing and helping James off his back and supporting him while he stood on his one good leg. They managed to help James into the back of the car where there was more room for him to stretch his right leg out. Without having to be asked, Tony got into the car and sat at the back beside James. Sally quickly drove the seven miles to the hospital. Throughout the journey Tony talked to James, keeping him calm and as comfortable as possible. Sally felt grateful for this so that she could just concentrate on the driving.

As they arrived at the hospital, before almost the car had fully stopped Tony jumped out, he ran inside the building and very quickly reappeared with a wheelchair. Fortunately the casualty department was not too busy so they did not have too long to wait. Tony stayed put in the waiting area while Sally accompanied James into the cubicle.

Up until now the white piece of cloth that Tony had used to cover the wound had been left undisturbed. This was now removed by the nurse who was there, assisting the doctor. James and Sally were both rather curious to look at the wound and were both expecting the worst. They both gave a small gasp, the doctor and nurse both presumed the couple were shocked at the sight of the wound, but in fact James and Sally were both taken aback because the wound was not as bad as they had expected.

They had both seen the wound soon after the accident. This wound though now seemed to be nowhere near as severe as they had imagined, the jagged edges of the wound were somehow straighter and cleaner and the wound did appear to be smaller. This wound did still need to have several stitches, but they both knew this wound would now heal quicker, and with less pain, than they had first thought. Both James and Sally knew this was because it had been tended to in the first instance by their own guardian angel. There was no way that they could tell this doctor and nurse the truth about the wound, they just let them get on with the stitching and the dressing of it. The doctor though did have to ask how James did get the cut, as of course he had to consider a tetanus injection. James just told him he did it while he was gardening, either way, however he got the injury, he still knew that he needed the tetanus injection. He just chose to be a bit sparing of the truth.

The suturing and dressing of the wound did not take too long at all. Sally was given instructions on basic care of the wound and when to go to see the practice nurse to have the stitches removed. James was then able to hobble back to the car and before long he was sitting comfortably at home with a cup of tea, and his leg well supported on a stool.

Tony came back in with them and was all too happy once again to be invited to share their evening meal. He left soon after the meal though, and as Sally saw him to the door she thanked him once again for his help. "I did not want to stay too late, I presume this could be a good time to tell James your special bit of news." Sally was taken aback with the excitement of the afternoon she had managed to put her bit of news to the back of her mind, but had to agree with Tony that this would be a good time to inform James. There was obviously now no doubt as to her pregnancy since Tony had had no problem guessing her news. He seemed to have confirmed the pregnancy for her, and of course now Tony knew her special piece of news she could not really keep this from James any longer.

CHAPTER THIRTEEN

Time seemed to pass by quickly in Marton cum Tiddleworth, and before they knew it, it was Christmas once again. It was hard to imagine they had lived in this lovely house and village for over a year. This Christmas though, James and Sally had invited both sets of parents to come and stay with them for a few days. It also seemed a good opportunity to share their news about the forthcoming grandchild, they had both managed to keep it a secret up until now.

Sally was off work for several days before Christmas so she had plenty of time to get organised. She was able to do last minute shopping and as much of the food preparation as possible. The fridge and freezer were both completely full. James was not as fortunate as Sally as he had to work right up to Christmas Eve. By the time he got home on Christmas Eve both their sets of parents were already there.

Earlier on in the day Sally had prepared a large meal, this only needed warming up, so she didn't have to spend too much time in the kitchen once their parents had arrived. When James came home from work he felt he really could now fully relax for a few days, the house looked lovely, so warm and cosy. They had decorated the house ready for Christmas a couple of weeks previously and it certainly did look grand.

They chose not go out after they had eaten, they all stayed in and relaxed. They enjoyed their meal and stayed for a while round the dining table after the meal, finishing the wine they had opened.

The following morning, Christmas day, they were all up at a reasonable time. Since there were no children to consider, they decided to put off the present opening until later. Together they had a leisurely breakfast and then set off for a brisk walk. There had been a sharp frost overnight. They all were well wrapped up, which was probably as well, they had only gone for a mile or so when it started to snow. It was only a light dusting of snow, but it made the village and surrounding countryside look even more picturesque.

It was just around lunchtime as they came to the end of their walk. None of them took much persuasion to stop at the Duck and Cow for a drink. Tony was helping out behind the bar and he greeted them all warmly as they went in. The pub was busy, but they were still able to find a table to accommodate them all, this table was conveniently situated not too far from the open fire. They stopped just long enough for one drink before they had to go out into the cold again and carried on the short walk back to James and Sally`s house.

Once they were back home Sally finished the preparations for the Christmas dinner. She had left the turkey on a low heat in the oven before they went out, and James had laid the table and now he helped with the vegetables. The house now had a rather delicious smell. There was not a great deal to do before the Christmas dinner was on the table, and Sally did have plenty of help.

The Christmas meal was a great success, the whole meal tasted delicious. Sally was really pleased with this, her first proper Christmas meal in their own home for both sets of parents, and with no major mishaps. Everyone rallied round and helped out, so Sally who had done all the planning and preparation for the meal did not feel in the least bit stressed.

It was sometime into the afternoon by the time they had cleared up from Christmas dinner. Everyone had chosen to have a cup of tea and they all then sat for some time slowly opening presents. No one felt like doing much else for the rest of the day, they were all too full to be bothered, so they just sat around the television watching an old film.

After the film had finished, no one was still in the slightest bit hungry but James did get up to put the kettle on again to make a warm drink. As he stirred and moved towards the kitchen, a sound from outside caught his attention. James went and opened the front door so he was able to hear the sound more distinctly. The sound James could hear was that of Christmas carols, it sounded too good for it to be a few children out carol singing, this did sound more like a full choir, but a full choir here in Marton cum Tiddleworth?

They had all been feeling quite lazy post-Christmas meal, now though they were able to rouse themselves enough to put on warm coats and head into the village centre to investigate. The singing was a full male choir, maybe about twenty of them, all stood in front of the pub. Sally, James and their parents were all stood completely mesmerised, the singing really was wonderful and such a sight to behold. Amongst the choir James and Sally had very quickly spotted Tony, he saw them and gave them a brief nod.

Most of the village had turned out to listen to this beautiful music. The choir sang several more carols before finishing with "Oh come all ye faithful." They encouraged everyone to join in with this. After the singing had ended Tony came over to speak to them for a few minutes, he clearly did not have much time. He was able to let James and Sally know they did this most Christmases and it did signify that all was well, in both this village at present and in the past. Tony mentioned that all of these fellow singers were friends of his, James and Sally though were sure they had not seen any of them here before, they were not from this village. Tony then wandered back to the rest of the choir.

Sally and James looked at each other. "Are we thinking the same thing? All of these singers in this choir, could they be angels? Wow." James and Sally had never realised, or even considered that Tony had any other angelic friends, let alone so many. They had both presumed he was unique.

During the singing none of them had realised how cold it was, now they all felt frozen. Fortunately Sally`s Dad had brought his wallet with him, it had been in his coat pocket, no one else had any money on them, they had all left the house quite quickly. Sally`s dad offered to buy them all another drink, since they were all stood there by the pub.

They were soon sat again by the roaring fire. The members of the choir had also come in for a quick drink. The pub really was busy by now. James and Sally`s parents all seemed relaxed and content, they were all enjoying the cosy atmosphere of the pub and it was such a lovely way to finish off Christmas Day. James and Sally though felt quite thrilled at the thought of being surrounded by so many angels. They did though appear to be ordinary men, there was nothing about them which made them stand out, but James and Sally still had to stop themselves from staring.

On the short walk back from the Duck and Cow Sally`s mum exclaimed about the sky. The bit of snow they had earlier had now stopped and it was a lovely crisp evening, very cold but such a clear sky. "Wow, just look up there," said Sally`s mum pointing upwards. There appeared to be a very bright star moving slowly across the sky. As they all looked up they realised this was not a solitary star but in fact there were several of them, all moving across the sky. It was as if these "stars" had all set off from more or less one point, not far from this village. They were now moving in different directions, radiating away from each other.

There was some discussion as to whether these really were stars, or if they were planes, this many though on Christmas day? Could it be that they were UFOs? James and Sally looked at each other and smiled. There was no way they were going to tell their parents that these "stars" really were heavenly bodies. It certainly did though put a magical end to this rather lovely Christmas Day.

The following day James parents had to leave, they were going off to visit more family. There was no particular need for them to rush off too soon, they were once again all able to have a leisurely breakfast together. Sally`s parent were staying another night. The snow that had fallen on Christmas Day had not been heavy at all, nothing like the previous Christmas. There were no concerns about the car being able to make it up the track and up on to the main road.

Before James parents left they had one last coffee, they were both a bit reluctant to go and leave this cosy house. "It has been a lovely Christmas," stated James mum, "it is a shame it has to end." "Before you go though, we do have one more rather special piece of news to share with you." Sally could not put off their news any longer, "How would you all feel about being grandparents? Our baby is due sometime toward the beginning of June"

Naturally their parents were thrilled, "well that really is the icing on the cake, as if this Christmas wasn't lovely enough." There were hugs and kisses all round and then very reluctantly James parents did have to go, they were expected at James brothers house for lunch. "Can we tell him your news?" asked James mum.

Once they had gone Sally`s mum put the kettle on again. Sally felt as if she had already drunk loads of fluids over the last day or so, the kettle seemed to have been constantly on. Sally`s parents were only staying for one more day, but Sally knew that during this time her mother would fuss over her. "Make the most of it," said James, "you will be back at work before you know it and rushed off your feet."

Twenty four hours later James and Sally were once again back by themselves again. It had been good having a full house over Christmas, but James, Sally and the house itself all seemed to breathe a sigh of relief when they were on their own again.

They had not made any specific plans, a few days later, to celebrate the New Year, so they celebrated this quietly, at the Duck and Cow. It felt good to be celebrating 2006. The previous year had been good, with everything that had happened, but they both knew that 2006 would be even better, particularly with the eager anticipation of the new baby. They both also wondered if there were any more surprises that could happen in this magical village, surely not. Even if there were no more magical surprises though they were both very content living here.

CHAPTER FOURTEEN

Soon enough the winter break came to an end and both James and Sally were back at work. Sally found she was more tired this half term, but otherwise she was feeling well. All of her colleagues at school were very pleased to hear her news. She decided though to leave it a bit longer until she told the children in her class.

The New Year had started cold and frosty, then one weekend they both woke up to find a light dusting of snow. This time, though, it had been forecast. It was not only their village that had had some snow. Sally was quite relieved when the snow had come over the weekend, she did not have to go out anywhere and had a large pile of books to mark, she now had a good excuse to stay inside. Sally took the pile of books, with a mug of coffee, into the study. She planned to spend the morning there.

Neither James nor Sally had ventured into the old world for a month or so. James found himself restless on this day with Sally busy, he was very keen to go on another adventure. He was curious to know how the weather was over there, if they were also having snow, he wanted to know how life was on the farm, and also if there was any news in general from the village of one hundred years ago.

With Sally's blessing, James wrapped up warm, put on a sturdy pair of walking boots and set off. Once he entered the world of 1906 James was not disappointed. The weather here was more or less the same as the weather that he had left behind. It was cold and crisp with a clear blue sky. It was not snowing, but they had had snow, there was an inch or two of lying snow here.

James walked over to the farm to meet Ted, Ted took a bit of locating, but James found him eventually in the large barn. He was not alone, Tony was with him. They were just clearing up after milking. James was relieved to know that he had timed the trip just right so he did not feel obliged to help with the milking. "We were both going to have a walk round the boundary of the farm, we need to make sure the fencing is in good order, that it will stand up to the rest of the winter. I don't want any livestock escaping. We would both be glad of the company if you would like to join us?" James was more than happy for the walk. They set off on their stroll around the farm, Ted stopping from time to time to look at the fencing. There were a few minor repairs necessary, that the three of them were able to do right there and then. The fence was mostly intact but it was rather worn.

"I did want to ask you," said James turning to Tony. "The choir at Christmas, I presume they were all friends of yours? Where did they all come from?" "They actually all live reasonably close, within about a fifty mile radius. We don't just sing here, but try to share some of the Christmas spirit in several other villages as well. All of these angels have their own communities to look after."

"Does every village or town have its own angel, and if so how come I have never met one before?" "Most areas do have their own guardian angel, unfortunately, there is just not enough of us to be everywhere that is needed. The majority of people do not know their own guardian angel, there are only a few small close knit communities, like this one, where the angel is known. This community though, as I am sure you have realised, is rather special.

The choir of angels get together to rehearse about once a month. We tend though to perform in front of a larger audience, only once a year, usually at Christmas. It is only this village that does know what we are when we are not singing, anywhere else we are just a male voice choir." "You certainly did sound heavenly, if you will pardon the pun. Sally and I, and our family were all very impressed."

They had, by now had completed their walk around the farm. Ted had stopped a few times to do a few quick, temporary repair jobs. James realised though time was getting on. He did not like to leave Sally for too long, he did now feel very protective of her. As they were heading off back to the farm, they saw, just a few yards away from them, what James at first thought was a swarm of insects. This could not be so though, it was too cold. It looked almost like a small cloud, maybe not a swarm of insects, this was too attractive. This "cloud" contained many pretty iridescent colours, lovely pastel shades of pale yellow, turquoise, lilacs and many other colours. As they got closer, this cloud seemed to shimmer and sparkle. James was mesmerised, his eyes were drawn to this attractive spectacular.

After a little while though, James did look away and looked towards Tony for some enlightenment as to what this was. Tony, of course was not at all surprised by this rather attractive sight. "Ah, fairy dust, it is supposed to bring you both good health and happiness if you walk through it. It is a shame that Sally is not here with us."

"How often does this occur, and does it only happen here?" "Oh, you come across it now and again, usually of course when the fairies are around." James looked astonished. "Real fairies, surely not?" "You only get to see the fairies if you believe in them. You must be at least some way to believing, or you would not otherwise get to see the fairy dust. I am sure some time, not too long ago, you must have also had your doubts about the existence of angels?"

"Can you only see this fairy dust here in this spot and at this time?" James wanted to know. "No, if you are in the right place and at the right time you can see the fairy dust in quite a few places. The fairies obviously prefer the countryside. You would never find any fairies living in the city. The weather also has to be right. They don't come out if it is raining. They usually seem to like bright sunny spots, they don't like extremes of temperature, like us I guess. It is a bit unusual to see them today, I would have thought it was a bit too cold for them. Fairies can only be seen by a person if they truly believe in them. If you keep an open mind though, you never know, you might get to see one, maybe even in your own garden. They always seem to be quite content there."

James could not wait to get home to tell Sally. Despite what Tony had said about this dust being lucky, James was reluctant to walk through the fairy dust. He did not want to disturb this beautiful shimmering cloud. He did put out his hand to tentatively touch it. The dust did not feel of anything, it just hung in the air and floated around James hand.

James stood and watched the dust for a few more minutes. He was reluctant to go, but was also excited about the thought of going home to tell Sally. As he stood there the dust started to fade and then disappeared completely. James looked disappointed. "Don't be too upset, you will get to see this again," Ted reassured him. "My children just love seeing the fairy dust. It will appear again soon, when you are least expecting it, maybe as Tony said, you may see it in your own garden."

James did go home then. He was certain that Sally would believe him, after so many other strange things had happened in this village, why not fairies as well. James was right, Sally was not unduly surprised. "In fact," said Sally, "I may have seen something like that already in the garden. A few months or so ago, on a nice day in autumn, I was hanging out the washing. I could see, not that far from me, something that looked like dragonflies. They looked as if they had left something behind, something like a colourful dust. The dust stayed around for only a few moments after the dragonflies, or fairies, had gone. They were all gone in a few minutes. I forgot to mention it."

"If you had been able to have had a closer look," said Tony, who had come back with James, "than you may have seen that they were not dragonflies, but fairies." "How can they have been fairies," replied James, "you said that you had to believe in fairies to see them?" Sally laughed at this. "How can I possibly be a junior school teacher, and not believe in fairies. I can`t wait to see them again, I will certainly take more notice next time."

Only a few days later both James and Sally were leaving the house, to set off to work, at the same time. As they were leaving the front door, they could not help notice that it was a lovely morning. The sky was blue and the morning had a lovely, fresh feel to it, too good really to have to be going to work. As they paused briefly to take in the beautiful morning they noticed just a few yards in front of them, just hovering over some flowers was what looked to be about three or four dragonflies.

They both crept quietly over to them in order to have a closer look. The "dragonflies" did not go, but stayed hovering in the same place. James and Sally were able to have a good look. As they did look it became apparent that the dragonflies were indeed fairies, with small dainty faces.

Neither James or Sally really had time to watch this pretty sight, they both should have been getting on to work. How though could they not stop for just a few more moments and watch, it was certainly a great way to start the working day.

The fairies did not seem at all disturbed by the presence of James and Sally, they were gently flitting around. James and Sally were able to get close enough to have a good look at their first real encounter with the fairies. The fairies had very delicate, but perfectly formed human faces. They each had, of course, a set of wings, nothing like the wings of Antonio, but each of these wings were in a lovely delicate pastel colour. Their wings were beating very fast as the fairies hovered around.

Something then seemed to disturb the fairies, or they had somewhere else to go. Together they gently and gracefully fluttered away out of the garden. "It is probably as well they have gone, that was quite amazing, but we both really should be going off to work. Hopefully we will see them again."

James and Sally set off on their own separate ways to work. They both did manage to concentrate at work, but their thoughts, of course kept going back to the lovely sight of the fairies.

CHAPTER FIFTEEN

A few weeks after the encounter with the fairies, James attempted to visit the old Marton cum Tiddleworth. Over on his side of the village the weather had been rather dull, it had been cloudy all day with no sign that the sun would emerge. James though found he was barely able to step out across to the other side. He had only opened the door to this other world, taken one step, when a dense fog hit him. This fog though felt different to any other fog James had previously encountered. It was only natural to expect a drop in temperature of a degree or two with a fog, but this felt like a huge drop. James was wearing Jeans and a T shirt with a fleece, but the cold hit immediately, penetrating right through the layers of his clothing.

James took a step or two back into his own world and felt the immediate warmth. There was something else though about this fog. Any normal, relatively dense fog, could feel almost sinister, but somehow this fog was different, it had a real menacing feel about it. James stood for a while in his world, watching the dense mist swirl around, it felt very dark and so unwelcoming.

James had felt a feeling of fear during the short period he had been stood in the fog. Now he shook himself, how could anyone be afraid of fog, especially when you are only walking in it, into this pleasant and friendly village? Fog can often pose a problem when out driving, particularly on a fast motorway, but not out here in the countryside, with no cars around. James knew there should be nothing to be afraid of. To prove himself right he took a few steps forward, closing the door to his world behind him.

James regretted this decision straight away. It was crazy, there should be nothing to be afraid of, but afraid he certainly was. It remained so cold. James could barely see a thing. There was nothing to orientate him to this world, which by now should be so familiar. James knew if he was not careful, if he moved too far away from the door, than he could so easily be lost. It was hard to imagine that he could be lost out here, but he was beginning to realise he was putting himself in danger. He was in danger from the cold alone. He was certainly not adequately dressed for this extreme cold and his hands and feet were now starting to tingle.

James managed to retreat a few steps back and was able to find the door that led him to the safety of his own world. Sally was surprised to see him back so soon. "I need to ring Tony," he told her. "Is there a problem over there?" "I am not so sure, I don't really know if there is a problem or not, or simply a case of severe weather."

James went on to explain to Sally about the problem with the fog. "Mmm, maybe nothing to worry about," replied Sally, "but it would be interesting to hear what Tony has to say." Tony answered the phone after a couple of rings. James told Tony about the fog. Tony was round at their house in only a few minutes. He did not hang around but was keen to head straight away to the old village. James was not too keen to encounter the fog again, but he was also very curious to see indeed if there was anything amiss, so he could not resist accompanying Tony. James only had enough time to get a thick, warm jumper and he put this on under a more adequate coat.

The fog had not lifted, if anything it seemed even denser, and even more menacing. "We could do with walking over to the village, to see if everything is OK. I am sure the village will be fine, but I would like to go and see for myself. Would you still like to come along?" Tony could see the worried look on James face. "I did bring a torch," said James, "but I don't know if it will be of any use in this fog." James switched on the normally more than adequate torch, but it made no difference at all. The fog just reflected any light from the torch back. James could barely see Tony, but he still chose to go with him rather than admit to his fear and return to his own world.

"We will be OK," said Tony, "stay close by." They took just two or three steps forward, then James glanced at Tony in amazement. Tony was surrounded by a glow of light, this glow was much more adequate then James torch. The glow of light emanating from Tony was enough to light up a reasonable area around the pair of them. Tony also of course had a much better knowledge of the local area than James had, there was no chance that he would get lost. James was surprised however to see how quickly they managed to reach the village, not that much longer than usual.

The thick dense fog had not lifted at all, it was just as bad here in the village. Although James was feeling much more reassured by following Tony with his amazing aura, he was by now chilled right through and was beginning to be worried about any other strange encounter or event that they might come across.

In the village they were greeted by a rather worried looking Ted. "Our unwelcome visitor has returned back to the village. Already the cows appear to be ailing and the hens have not laid a single egg all week." "You should have let me know sooner, I had no idea. You have James to thank that I am here today otherwise the situation could have become much worse."

James looked from one worried face to the other with no idea of what was going on. It did though sound rather sinister. Their own village of Marton cum Tiddleworth was always so pleasant and this same village, set one hundred years previously, also usually had such a lovely atmosphere. James could not imagine anything too bad happening in either village.

Tony explained to James exactly what the problem was. Any time travel that occurs anywhere does so usually against nature. "The time travel you are aware of, seems to be accepted by nature, probably because we try to limit it and try not to change anything in the world which is not our own. When we do time travel here we do everything that we can to preserve life as it is in this land. The time travel can only occur by that small area next to your house as there is only a thin veil there in-between these two worlds. No one knows why it happened there and why it happened at all. We are very fortunate that it did occur there. Unfortunately though, there is also another thin veil in-between this village and the same village one hundred years even further back. There is a certain force, one that is not very welcome, and from time to time tries, and sometimes succeeds, in getting through, not from our village of Marton cum Tiddleworth as we know it, but from another one hundred years back in the year 1806, to here at this time of 1906.

As far as I am aware this very rarely happens, but the last time that it did happen, it did so with dire consequences. Two of the villagers, from two hundred years in our past, had managed to somehow unlock the veil between these two worlds and had time travelled forward one hundred years to this particular time. The time travel did not affect them in anyway, but it did cause an imbalance in nature. Both of those villagers from two hundred years ago were carrying a disease that they passed on to this village.

Some of the villagers of 1806 had previously become aware of the chance to time travel, but had not chosen to experiment with it, that is, until a serious disease struck their own village. They had tried to escape the outbreak of this quite serious illness in their world, but in escaping, they had managed unwittingly to bring the infection into this same village, one hundred years ahead of their time.

It was quite catastrophic. Many of these villagers here in 1906 caught the disease and nearly half of the village was wiped out. I had thought I had put all the measures in place that was necessary in order to stop this time travel ever occurring again."

Turning to Ted, Tony asked him if he was aware of seeing anyone from the village of 1806 appearing here in this village of 1906. Ted looked thoughtful. "I have not seen any strangers here recently. I am sure anyone from the village would have said if a stranger did appear. The last stranger that came to our village was James." Ted said this nodding over to James with a half-smile.

"We will have to have a look around," said Tony wandering over towards the farm. James wondered what on earth they were actually looking for, but he did not like to ask. He was certainly not yet familiar enough with most of the people in this village to be able to tell if they were locals or not.

James tagged on behind Tony and Ted and tried to look as if he was helping. It was good to be moving again. The fog had not lifted and was as dense as ever, it was still very cold.

They wandered over to look at the cows in the field, even James could tell that they were not right, they seemed somehow to be very listless. Tony looked deep in thought. "There is not much we can do here, let's go to the Duck and Cow and get warm, it should be open by now." The pub was indeed open with a hearty fire burning. The three of them sat with a pint each mulling over the problem, not that James was doing much mulling. He knew so little about this problem which was happening here, in this period of time, let alone on how on how to help solve it. James could tell from Tony and Ted that this problem was indeed very serious but he was in no position to help and he felt a bit useless. Despite the warm fire, the atmosphere in the pub did seem rather gloomy. There were not too many other people in there, but they all looked very troubled.

"When we have finished this pint and got warm, we will go and have a look at the point of entry between the two worlds. I am not so sure though if I will be able to tell if there has been any tampering with the crossing." James felt that Tony seemed as much a loss over knowing what to do as he was.

They finished their drinks and James followed Ted and Tony to what he presumed was the point of entry between the world of 1806 and 1906. He had assumed it would be in more or less the same place as where he travelled in-between the two worlds and was surprised to find that it was in another part of the village. This time it was much closer to the village centre, it was along a wall, James had not really taken any notice of this wall before. It was situated somewhere in-between the blacksmiths and the small village school. "Wouldn't anyone have noticed if someone had entered the village just here, particularly a stranger?" "You would think so," replied Tony, grimly. "I don't know how they are getting through."

"Has anyone ever been to pay them a visit?" James asked. He had no idea if it was possible to time travel in this direction, he did know it was certainly not a good idea for a villager from 1906 to travel to 2006. "Aye, I have been across," replied Tony. "It took quite a toll on him," butted in Ted, "he was not gone for long but he looked ill on his return." "I am not sure if I want to repeat the experience, but it may be the only way we can prevent further harm coming to this village."

"What happened when you went the last time?" asked James. "It was some time ago when a few of the men came across and unfortunately brought the disease we mentioned. I knew that something had to be done before more people came across. If we did not do anything to stop them then this entire village could have been wiped out.

I managed to cross the one hundred year gap back in time and found several of the more senior men in the village. I did my best to explain about the havoc they were causing here. They didn't seem to realise that any of their fellow villagers had been actually time travelling, it was rather hard to explain to them about this concept. The few men who had done the time travelling were also unsure in exactly what they were doing. They just seemed to think they had slipped through a gap in the wall and were visiting another village of their own time. It had not occurred to any of them at the time that they had not walked any distance at all in-between the two villages, and therefore it had to be the same village. They could not see the familiarities of this village and their own, that all the buildings were very much the same and also in the same place. They did not also notice this village of 1906 was more advanced than their own. They just seemed to think by coming here, they were avoiding catching the disease in their own village.

I think I did eventually manage to persuade them that by crossing through this barrier they were causing a lot of trouble for their future generations. It was hard to get them to understand. They, seemed to live for the present, I guess understandably. They didn't have the foresight at all to realise what they were doing with the time travelling, that this could possibly have a big impact on future generations, or even on the lives of their own children, that by travelling here, they could not actually prevent themselves getting infected, but they were actually managing to spread the disease further. Fortunately though, after I had spoken to them, they did stop the time travel, they no longer crossed the gap between the two worlds. Even more fortunately the disease then did stop, naturally, without any more deaths.

Anyway back to the present. We still don't know what to do about this problem. The villagers of one hundred years ago did, at the time, promise not to return to this village of the 1900`s. I did manage to persuade them that it could be dangerous for them and also dangerous for future generations. That was a few years ago, it was in fact 1801 then, they could easily by now have forgotten their promise, maybe there have been other changes in the village. It was a few of the older men I spoke to back then. Their agreement about time travel may not have been passed on or it could have been disregarded. There is only one thing for it, I will have to go back there again."

A dark look passed over Ted's face, he did appear to be very concerned. "Could I come with you?" James was by now well aware of the danger, but he also so wanted to be part of the excitement and did want to do his bit and try to help. Tony thought over this request. "I am really not so sure about that, I wouldn't want you to risk your own health by accompanying me, you do have to consider Sally and the baby. I am quite certain by now you know I am very lucky to have my own extra protection, that only I in this village am privileged to have, hopefully, because of it, I will be OK.

There is no point in delaying this venture any further, I may as well go now. The situation here will not get any better the longer that we sit here procrastinating." Tony bent down to where there was another crescent moon and star shapes in the brick work of the wall. He pressed it gently and as if by magic a door opened up in between the two worlds. Tony entered this world with a good luck from Ted. The door slowly closed behind Tony.

"How long is he likely to be?" "Who knows," replied Ted, "I only hope he does not come to any harm. He is certainly a rock for both of our villages, this present one as I know it, and of course for yours as well. Anyway we cannot stand here all day, he could be some time yet. Our waiting around will not bring him back any quicker. There is always plenty of work to be done on the farm, are you busy, do you have to get back to Sally or is there any chance of a hand?" "No problem" replied James. "I have some spare time and would like to be around when Tony does return." James followed Ted away from the wall and towards his farm. James hoped that they were not going over to the farm just in time to milk the cows.

Across on the other side of the wall, in the village of 1806 Tony noticed that the fog was just as dense here. He had crossed over close to the centre of the village. There were a few villagers around. They gave Tony a polite nod and a curious stare. The people who lived in this village of 1806 were not used to strangers and, just as he had actually done, Tony did appear to have come from nowhere. Tony knew that he would have to act quickly, the rumour that there was a stranger in the village would soon spread. Tony knew that he was more than likely to have to face some hostility and the longer he delayed the more this hostility would grow.

Tony knew that probably the most appropriate place to start his search, and find the best person to talk to, was more than likely to be in the village pub. Tony took a stroll over to the Duck and Cow, the pub still had this name. Tony always kept some "old" money in his pocket, money from before decimalisation that he was able to use to buy a drink with, usually in the Duck and Cow of 1906. Tony also always kept some money hidden deep in his pocket that was dated pre 1806. Even Tony though today was surprised to see just how cheap the pint of beer was in 1806.

Tony asked for his drink and then glanced around. He saw several sets of eyes on him. Even for Tony this felt somewhat uncomfortable, he was very much the stranger in town. One of the older men came over and shook Tony's hand. "Hello there, it is has been some time since we last met." Tony realised this was one of the men that he had met with previously, the last time he was here. Tony remembered him, not his name, but that fortunately previously when he was here before, he had taken him seriously about the dangers of time travel.

"Hello, how is life with you?" "Mustn't grumble" came the reply. "The farm is doing well. At least it was until this fog came down. It has been with us for a few days now, it is so dense. I don't remember having fog before like this, that has lasted so long. The livestock also, since this fog came, seemed to be suffering. It has made both animals and people so tired as if no one can be bothered."

"Would you happen to know if anyone has travelled across the time gap?" Tony did his best to keep his voice down, he had to presume very few of these villagers would know about the time travel, and Tony wanted to keep it that way. The fewer people that knew, then the fewer temptations there would be to go exploring. "As far as I know no one has dared to go across the gap again. I am one of the few who does know about the secret of the wall. I have sworn to myself that I will take this secret to the grave." Tony was quite certain Henry was telling the truth, Tony had somehow managed to remember his name while they were talking.

"Has anything else strange happened in the village that you know of? This fog is not just here, it is just as bad in this village of 1906. Something must have happened to upset the balance between these time periods. I am sure if we do not do anything to find the reason for this weather, it will only get worse. Like here, in 1906 the fog and the whole atmosphere is affecting the livestock. The fog is so thick, and the weather so cold, it does make it difficult for people to go about their everyday lives. It will not be long before milk production is down."

"You are right, the wife did say the hens are not laying, we only just have enough eggs for ourselves, and not had any left to sell. Everyone seems to be in poor spirits, it is not only the animals. The bad feelings here though could also be caused by the missing child."

Tony was alerted at this news and wanted to know more. Henry informed Tony about a boy aged seven who had been playing by the village well. "He was seen climbing into the well and down a few steps of the metal ladder by another child. He has not been seen since. It happened two days ago, there has been no sight of the poor young lad since then. The child's mother is frantic."

"Has the well been explored?" Tony wanted to know. "Aye," replied Henry, "it certainly has. The boy's dad of course went down the well steps as soon as he heard that his son was missing, but there was no sight of the lad. He climbed down as far as the water and then went into the water itself. He has been back down there a few times since. He is certainly not wanting to find his son's body, but after this time it seems to be the only thing that could have happened to the boy. The poor lad probably went down the well for a bit of a lark and must have drowned down there, maybe lost his grip on the ladder."

"Have other places been searched?" asked Tony. "Could the boy have perhaps climbed out of the well again and gone hiding somewhere, in the woods maybe?"

"We have thought of that. We have searched everywhere. He is just nowhere to be found. The family have a sheepdog, and the dog and the lad were close, if you know what I mean. The dog has fair pined for the lad ever since he has gone missing. You would have thought if the lad were to be found anywhere then the dog would have found him by now. The dog though does keep walking back to the well and whining. It sure does look as if the poor mite has drowned down there.

No one will use that well now. Some folk want it covering up so that no other child can go down there, but his poor Mam and Dad keeping hoping that one day he will climb out of it again. This sure would be a miracle. We just keep hoping at least that his body will turn up so that he can have a proper burial."

"Can I have a look in the well?" asked Tony. "Aye you can look for nowt, I am sure we have all had a good look and it just ain't going to bring the poor lad back."

Tony had by then finished his pint. Tony and Henry got up together and walked over to the old village well. "Where does everyone go now for their water, I presume no one now uses this well?" "There is another well on the outskirts of the village. It is not too far away, but a long way if you have water to carry and you have to do that trip a few times a day."

By now they had reached the well. They both peered down into the darkness. The old metal ladder was there, it did look sturdy enough. Henry could tell what Tony was thinking. "The ladder is strong enough, but it is so slippery, you will have to watch your footing. A few of the villagers have been down the ladder to see if we could rescue the lad, but there is nothing down there, only water."

"I shall go down though" said Tony, "you just never know what I might find." "Please yourself," replied Henry. He clearly thought Tony was wasting his time and interfering with what they had already tried.

Tony took a deep breath and climbed over the shallow wall and on to the top of the ladder. It was certainly gloomy down there in the well, made even gloomier by the persistent fog and penetrating cold. Even Tony had no idea what he was going to achieve by climbing down there, but he was at a loss as to know what else to do. He very much wanted to help not only this village, but also to improve the weather in 1906. Tony though had no idea where to start looking for the boy.

Tony climbed down and down towards the end of the ladder. When Tony was close to the water, feeling even colder than ever, he suddenly noticed a change in the wall of the well. The wall had, up to here, been a solid circular wall forming this well. Here though, near the water, part of the wall went in, almost in the shape of a window. Tony was able, with some caution, to step off the ladder on to the ledge formed by the change in the brickwork.

It was very dark down here, there was now no natural light at all coming in. Tony though was able to create his own light, even this was not too bright, but was enough for him to see in the gloom. "Well, well," said Tony to himself, unaware of the unfortunate use of words. "I certainly didn't know about this." Not far from Tony's feet, where he was stood somewhat precariously on the narrow ledge, there was a crescent moon and star shape on one of the bricks.

Tony bent down and pressed this brick. The wall in front of him opened. It opened into a small dark room. Tony

193

had not been aware that this room existed. The room was in complete darkness. Tony though was just about able to see by his own light, so he could have a good look around this small room. The room unfortunately though was quite empty.

Tony had been hoping to find the child here. This room felt so cold and dank. Tony shuddered, all he wanted to do was to get out as quickly as he could, even though the weather outside had been far from good it was certainly preferable to this cold, dark dampness down here.

Before Tony could leave this well he felt he should look around some more, in case there was something that was missing. He did think maybe this room could lead on to another, but there was no evidence for this, there were no more bricks with the familiar star and crescent moon. Despite the cold and gloom Tony had a good look round before he left. As he came out of this cold strange room Tony considered climbing down further into the well, but he really couldn't see though what it would achieve apart from getting himself soaking wet.

Tony was now standing near the bottom of the ladder, he was so close to the water. He had one last look around, but there was nothing there. He was very disappointed he had not found the boy, but he did feel though the answer to the puzzle of the missing boy lay in that room that he had just chanced upon.

Shivering, Tony climbed up the slippery, but solid, rungs of the ladder. Henry was still waiting anxiously for him. "You were gone for some time, I was getting worried for your safety. I presume there was no sight of the lad." "No sorry," replied Tony. "I might have an idea though, I first have to return to my world."

Henry did not look convinced. He just shrugged. He could not understand why climbing down into the well, unless to recover the body, could help at all. There really was nothing to see down there.

Tony left him and returned to the village of Marton cum Tiddleworth of just one hundred years ago. The well still existed here in this village. It had been filled in some time between 1906 and 2006. Tony realised the only chance they had of finding the child was here in this village, and at this time in history. When he returned, James was not around, Tony guessed that he would probably be helping out on the farm. Tony went off to explore the well by himself.

Fortunately for Tony there wasn't anyone else around. Tony was able to jump up on to the wall and down the metal ladder without being seen. It didn't really matter if anyone did see him, but it could slow down the search if Tony had to stop and give an explanation. These metal steps were also very slippery, but fortunately still felt quite sturdy. Tony clung on as tight as he could.

Tony descended about as far as he had done previously and there, in the same place was the alteration in the brickwork, there was the same kind of ledge, it obviously was the same ledge. Tony had climbed down here in the dark, any light at all came through from the top of the well. This light though now failed. Once again Tony cast an aura of light around him.

Tony climbed off the ladder and on to the seemingly narrow ledge. He could see the same star and crescent moon. Tony bent down cautiously to press these. Once again the wall opened into the dark room. This time though the room wasn't quite empty. There crouched in one corner, in an apparently poor state was a small boy. This had to be the missing boy.

Tony was really amazed and delighted to see him still alive. Tony had no idea how he had got here, was it possible that there was another entry point here, in this well between the two worlds? Now though was not the time to uncover this mystery. Tony bent down to the small boy, he did not want to frighten him, but he did need to get him out of this cold dark hole and back to his mother. Tony let his wings unfurl. He talked gently, soothingly to the boy. Tony now realised he did not even know the boy's name, he had not thought to ask before he set off to look for him, Henry had certainly not mentioned his name. Tony crept closer to the boy and wrapped him in his wings. The boy did not protest, he was probably far too weak to know what was happening.

Tony was able to keep the boy safe in his wings, which also served the purpose of providing some much needed warmth. Slowly and carefully, with the boy wrapped gently in his wings, Tony climbed up the ladder of the well. When Tony got up to the top of the well James was there. James had finished helping on the farm, he had not really done very much work on the farm, he found that he could not put his mind to helping, he only wanted to know what was happening to Tony in the year 1806. James was not too far from the well as Tony climbed out, holding his precious bundle. The poor little boy still looked very cold and understandably rather ill. Tony knew most importantly he would probably be in need of a drink, he must surely be very dehydrated if he had been missing for two days. Tony had no time to waste, he knew the boys only chance of recovery was to get him home, to his own time, as soon as possible.

It wasn't too far to the wall, where Tony could once more cross the time gap. Tony walked rapidly to the wall, with James following. James wanted very much to see if the boy was OK, but he knew better than to follow Tony back further in time. Tony crossed over into 1806 with the boy still secure in his wings. Tony had only stepped a short way into 1806 when he came across Henry.

Tony quickly showed him the boy and asked him to lead the way to the boy's house. The house was not too far away and fortunately the boy's mother was at home. His mother was, naturally delighted to see the return of her son, this soon turned to concern over the boy, as he did look so ill.

The boy's mother did not bat an eyelid when her son was returned to her by an angel, she was so pleased to have him back that she had hardly noticed Tony. The boy did seem to stir in Tony's arms as if he sensed the presence of his mother. Tony, and particularly his mother, fussed over the boy. They covered him with blankets, his mother built up the fire in the room. Slowly as the child became more alert, they were able to give him a few sips of fluids. In time the boys colour returned, he had been very pale, almost ashen, now there was a little more pink in his cheeks, he looked a slightly healthier colour.

While Tony and the boy`s mother were tending to the boy, the boy's father came in, along with his father there was also the dog, the one Henry had mentioned. Tony had by then discovered the lad was called Samuel. His father had been out on what of course had been another fruitless search for his son. Tony was very pleased to see the obvious joy shown by not only both the boy's parents, but also by the dog. Tony could see that Samuel was now recovering well, and did seem to be out of danger.

Tony took himself to the back of the room and allowed Samuels parents to take over the care. Quietly, without a word to the boy or his parents, Tony stepped outside to return to his own world. The thick fog was now starting to lift, there was still a lot of mist swirling around, but it did now have the promise of turning out to be a good day.

On his way back to the wall, and the village of 1906, Tony came across Henry. "I presume the poor wee mite did not survive than?" "I suggest that you go and pay the family a visit," Tony replied, nodding in the direction of the farm labourer's cottage he had just left. Tony took his leave of 1806 and travelled on to 1906 and went in search of James.

Tony soon found James, he was sat propping up the wall, more or less where he had left him some time previously. The fog had now completely lifted and just like 1806 the weather here had turned out to be very good. Together they made their way home, to Whisper Lane of 2006, where Tony was inevitably invited to share their evening meal. Sally was by now more than used to cooking an extra portion.

The weather here in 2006 had also improved. There had not been the dense fog here, but it had been rather dull and cloudy. When they got back home though, the clouds had lifted and the sun was shining.

CHAPTER SIXTEEN

Once the news of Sally's pregnancy was out she was able to go and have a chat with Wendy. Wendy was able to put Sally's mind at ease that time travel did appear to be safe when pregnant, she had sailed through her four pregnancies with no problems at all. "It is not exactly something you could discuss with the midwife," said Sally. "No, please don't even think about it, she would probably start to worry about your mental stability!" Sally was reassured over this, that she would still be able to time travel. Despite the reassurance though, Sally had already decided, maybe for the time being, time travel was something she would probably put on hold.

A couple of months later on a late Saturday afternoon in March, Sally was in her kitchen starting to prepare the evening meal. The day had started out very wet, but however the rain had stopped a couple of hours ago, and the weather had turned out to be pleasant. There had been no breeze earlier, Sally though could now hear the wind getting up. James had been outside, working in the garden and had come in for a warm drink. He also commented on the breeze. "There seems to be a bit of a wind getting up, but it only seems to be centred on our garden. There had been no forecast of a wind and outside the garden, further away the trees are barely moving at all."

Sally stopped what she was doing and went outside. The trees once again did seem to be whispering, as if they had a message to tell. Sally then realised she had never told James about the day he had had his accident on the farm, how she had received the warning. Sally went back inside to James, who was now putting the kettle on. He had taken off his outdoor shoes and looked as if he had stopped any work for the rest of the day. He looked up at Sally and saw the rather worried look on her face. "We have to phone Tony," announced Sally immediately reaching for the phone. James looked a bit puzzled, but didn't get the chance to ask just why they had to phone Tony. Sally explained again to Tony about the whistling noise again through the trees in their garden. "I will be over straight away."

They did not have long at all to wait for Tony to arrive. Sally used these few minutes to explain to James about how she had heard this sound before, and previously, not knowing what to do she had turned to Tony for help. "I had thought then, at the time when I had my accident, it was Tony's angelic instinct that brought him over to my rescue."

Once Tony arrived he wasted no time in setting off in the direction of the old outbuilding, he only paused long enough to suggest that James go with him but whatever the problem was over there he did not wish for Sally to come along, as they all may be in danger. "Just be careful, the pair of you." They probably didn't hear Sally as they left at such a speed, James appeared to be having some difficulty in keeping up with Tony.

As soon as James and Tony arrived in the old Marton cum Tiddleworth they immediately knew what the trouble was. They could see smoke billowing out from one of the barns on the farm. The smell of smoke hung in the air and they could even hear the crackle of fire, not to mention the rather harrowing sound of distressed animals. Together they hurried towards the barn which was on fire. There were already many people milling around there, Ted, Sadie and many farm labourers.

This barn had been full of hay and was now well alight. Everyone seemed to be rushing about trying to put the fire out, but they were certainly not very well organised, and in an effort to be quick they were constantly getting in each other's way and hence slowing down the process. Next door to this barn was another barn, which unfortunately at present was full of cows that had recently been brought in for milking.

The scene in front of James and Tony was of complete chaos. Tony strode over to farmer Ted who was looking very distraught. Tony had a few words with him and then with Ted's permission he took charge. A few minutes later, although the scene was still that of devastation, people began to become more organised, to work together, more as a team.

James was amazed at how easily Tony took control and how he seemed to think of everything. Christine and William were there of course, trying to help. Tony told Christine to take, not only the farm children, but several other children who had either come out of curiosity or who had come along in an effort to help, over to the school, away from any danger. He knew Christine would want to help here with the fire, but at present it was more important to keep the children away.

Tony turned next to James who was about to start carrying buckets of water to help quench the flames. "We are going to need more man power. Could you please go back to your house and ask Sally if she can get some more help. I am sure that Pete and Dave will help."

As James was hurrying back towards his own world, he could not help wondering if they should indeed be helping in the first place, let alone getting extra help. Wasn't this changing the course of history, just as Tony had warned them not to do, was it right that they could be slightly altering the course of history, or if they didn't help then lives could perish? James of course had to dismiss this thought. Now was not the right time to be considering this.

When James arrived home he quickly told Sally of the problem. "Please can you ring Pete and Dave and see if they can help." "No problem," replied Sally. "Would you like me to come and help as well?" "No, sorry you will have to stay here, it is too dangerous," with the message delivered James quickly returned to help with the fire.

The fire, when James returned, no more than ten minutes or so later, seemed to be just as fierce. Tony had organised a chain of people with buckets of water, and when James got closer he realised they were now making some head way with at least containing the fire. James went to join in the chain. Tony though had another job for him. "I am sorry to have to ask you to do this, but could you please help Sadie with the cows. They have to be moved back to the field, we cannot leave them in that barn, it is likely they would perish if we did." This was the last job that James wanted, but he could not protest. He also actually felt honoured that Tony had asked him, knowing Tony had enough faith in him to trust him with this task.

The cows had to be moved through a narrow side entrance in the smaller barn, where they had been taken to ready for milking not long before this horrific fire took hold. The herd now had to be led a long way round the farm, as far away from the fire as possible and back to their field. Their normal routine was certainly disturbed. The cows were fairly skittish, they were clearly bothered by the fire and presumably also were somewhat uncomfortable since they had not yet been milked. The task of milking the cows would now have to wait until later.

The cows were not so very easy to manage, but James followed Sadie's calm manner, and they did between them manage to return the cows to the field. As soon as they were back in the field the cows attention went straight back to grazing the rather lush grass. The cows were now far enough away from the fire not to be too bothered by it.

James was well aware that Sadie's apparent calmness must be on the surface. Deep down she surely must be in turmoil. This large barn fire had already lost them so much hay, as well as the barn itself. There was now also the concern that this fire, which was not yet under control, was very close to the actual farmhouse.

As soon as they had returned the cows to the field, ensuring the gate was securely fastened behind them, James and Sadie returned to the scene of the fire. It looked as if putting out this fire was going to be a massive task.

Tony had organised a small chain of people, passing buckets back and forth, from a nearby well. There was also a longer chain who were passing buckets of water taken from the village pond. Even some of the older children were helping by the pond. They were well away from any danger from the fire and they were working well under the supervision of Christine. Christine had left one of the more capable older girls in charge of the younger children in the school house.

James paused only for a short while wondering where he would be most useful. There were some large gaps in the longer chain of volunteer fire fighters. He felt he could be of use here, in an effort to make the gaps in this chain shorter and therefore more effective. He then looked over to the fire itself. The men working closest to the fire looked worn out and not to mention extremely hot. James decided it would be best if went to help out here. Once there he took over from

Peter, who was very grateful for the chance of moving away for a while from the intense heat.

James quickly got into the rhythm of accepting a full bucket of water and then throwing this at the fire and then returning the empty bucket back along the chain. James gave a quick glance at the other labourers and realised it was more effective to throw the water as low as possible, rather than throwing it randomly at the flames.

The heat was fierce but with the constant action James was able to put the heat to the back of his mind, and worked as hard as he could. James could see that it would take some time yet to quell this fire, but the other farm buildings, including the farmhouse did at least now appear to be all safe. With a bit of luck the only thing that was likely to be lost in this fire was this barn of hay.

After what seemed like rather a long time Peter came back and took James place. He pushed James further down the chain, away from the intense heat of the fire. James was able to pause only for a second or two, but it gave him long enough to realise they were at last beginning to make some progress. The fire did now seem to be dying down very slowly. James could not be sure if this was through their efforts or if the fire was now starting to run out of fuel. Most of the hay now appeared to have gone, lost to the fire.

As James and Peter passed bucket after bucket of water back and forth to each other and then further up the line,

Peter commented they were now winning the battle to put out the fire. "There is still a long way to go yet though." "I have never grafted so hard before in my life," replied James. "Ah, you soft office workers. What we could do with now though is a bit of divine intervention," said Peter nodding over towards Tony.

Peter obviously knew Tony better than James did. The only person that James had talked to about Tony's extraordinary powers was Sally. He had never had the courage or found the right moment to ask Tony himself outright, or even for that matter any of the other villagers, exactly what Tony was able to do. James often did wonder, and particularly at this moment, just how much power Tony did have. Surely Tony wasn't capable of putting out this fire or he would have done so already.

James had heard a few murmurs about the probable cause of the fire. He was already aware that in this village, they had been having a rather unseasonable hot dry spring. James had experienced this for himself when he had ventured across only a week or two ago. Earlier on today though there had been a storm, only a very short sharp one, with a very brief period of rain. The storm had moved on as quickly as it had arrived, but there had been some lightening, and it was this lightening the villagers thought to have been the cause of this hay fire.

While they were working hard, as if the heat from the fire was not enough, the weather had returned to the heat wave of the last few weeks. The brief storm had certainly not lasted and had done nothing to lower the temperature. James had to put thoughts of heat to the back of his mind. The first thing that he intended to do, when he eventually got home was to have a long, cold shower. It was hard to imagine ever feeling the cold again.

As James continued to work hard, he did start to notice some small changes taking place in the weather. The flames from the fire were still very bright, but from where James was stood he was able to get a brief glimpse of the sky. The sky had previously been an uninterrupted blue, now though it did appear to be getting darker. James was well aware any rain at all would bring a welcome relief. A drop of rain would not be enough to put out this fire, but it would certainly feel good on the skin. The sky though did not look dark enough for rain, it was probably only a passing cloud.

James mind went back to the job in hand. He was becoming aware of how exhausted he was, but there was no way he could stop now and have a rest. James had no idea how much time had passed since he had arrived back in this Marton cum Tiddleworth after going back to his house to summon help. It must have been a couple of hours at least, but he had completely lost track of time. As well as being so hot he was also feeling very thirsty, he did not want to stop though, not even long enough for a drink.

James did manage to pause for a very brief moment or two, and he stood up straight so he could stretch his back.

He glanced up at the sky again and was surprised to see how dark it had now become. He motioned up to the sky, pointing this out to Peter. "Aye, I had noticed, it looks as if the divine intervention has at last arrived!" With this comment James felt the wonderful experience of the first drops of rain on his skin. He had never before felt so pleased to feel rain. He remembered about how often in the past he had moaned about rain, never again.

The first few drops of rain became gradually heavier. Everyone stopped working for a short while, to rest and to watch and feel this welcome rain falling. The fire had by now slowly started to die down, with all their effort, with all the buckets of water that had been poured on to it by the farm labourers and villagers. This rain though, which was now very heavy, did seem to be having a very beneficial effect on the fire. Everyone was able to step back away now from the remains of the barn and watch the fire slowly die down even further. Christine and Sadie had by now taken all of the children inside, including those who had been helping with the fire, out of the pouring rain. It was now safe to go back into the farmhouse, there was no chance now the fire could spread, it was well under control.

Tony had wandered over to Peter and James. "The rain certainly took its time in arriving," commented Peter to Tony, almost accusingly. "At least it has now arrived, I cannot control everything. Thanks though anyway to you both. I am sure you have both earned a few free pints in the pub the next time you happen to be passing this way."

"Talking of which," said Dave, striding over. "I think we deserve a drink right now, I could sure do with a pint to quench my thirst." "Isn't the pub closed though, what with everyone helping out with the fire?" enquired James. "It may be closed, but I can still get in," announced Dave, producing the key. "How come you have a key for this pub?" James was curious to know. "Easy," replied Dave, with a grin, "it is the same key, the lock has not changed for the last one hundred years."

The four of them, James, Peter, Tony and Dave walked away from the farm and across to the pub. The fire had by now almost died down. Farmer Ted and several others stayed behind by the barn to make sure there would be no more sparks which could reignite the fire. The rain though was still falling and was still heavy. James, who had been so hot not too long ago was now soaked to the skin and had started to shiver.

Dave put his key in the lock and let them into the pub. He then headed to the back of the bar. James realised he was almost as familiar with this bar as he was with his own. This pint of beer was very welcome. James would have loved to have stayed there for some time and certainly would have appreciated at least one more pint. He couldn't stay though, he was becoming increasingly uncomfortable in his wet clothes. He also needed to get home to Sally, to let her know what had been happening, she was probably rather worried.

Before James got up to go he had to ask about the loss of hay to the farm. Tony replied, "It will be somewhat of a blow to Ted, but he will more than likely get some help from the neighbouring farms, it is surprising how they all rally round. I am sure that Ted will have helped with his neighbours in the past."

By now they had all finished their drinks. Dave left the glasses at the back of the bar and locked the door behind them. He need not have bothered doing this. They had only gone a few yards when a few of the locals and of course the real pub landlord came along, all in need of a drink. They all looked even ruddier in the face than usual, with a few singed eyebrows.

James had to return to Sally. He walked back with Tony and Dave. Before they returned to 2006 though, they made a small diversion to check on the fire. All that remained of the fire was some smouldering embers. The rain had now eased off, but hopefully it would continue to drizzle for some time to come.

There were only a handful of people standing by the remains of the barn, many of the others, who had come to help, now had to return back home and to their own lives. Ted was still there though of course. "One of us at least, will keep watch throughout the rest of the evening and also through the night. There has certainly been a lot of damage, but it could have been a lot worse."

As James, Tony and Dave walked back towards home, James again expressed his concern over Ted's loss. "He will manage," replied Tony. "He always manages to fight back no matter what bad luck is thrown his way. I am sure he will be OK and will get some help."

Sally had been kept busy while the men had been away helping with the fire. She had once again prepared a large meal with plenty to spare for Tony. Dave was also invited to stay and eat with them, however he had to decline the offer, as he had to get back to his own pub. Sally, naturally, was very keen to hear about the fire, she had been worried about the damage that could have occurred and was very relieved to hear that no one was seriously injured.

CHAPTER SEVENTEEN

A few weeks after the fire, James and Sally met up with Tony in the Duck and Cow. The conversation, of course, at first was about the fire, the devastation it had caused, but also how it could have been so much worse. James still couldn't get his thoughts around how much they should help in the old village and where they risked changing the course of history. James was going to broach the subject with Tony, but this particular evening he didn't get the chance. Tony had other matters on his mind.

Tony turned the discussion round to the fairies, how they were very special, how they were fortunate to have them in this village, that they brought not only good luck and good health to the village, but also peace and contentment. They all agreed it was a cheerful community, and one in which everyone did seem to enjoy good health, the villagers did seem to live to a good age. "Surely though having a guardian angel would help!"

Tony smiled at this, he then became more serious. He went on to explain he had heard of a proposed housing development. "The development would be built on a large piece of land on the edges of the village itself. The developers will therefore probably get permission for the build to go ahead. If it was to actually be in the village itself then they would not get planning permission, they would not be allowed to change the character of this village. Where they are proposing to build this new development, just outside the boundary, it shouldn't change the village as such, but the village will never be as peaceful again. I do also know the development will send the fairies away, they will only live in a quiet peaceful community where they are not disturbed, the proposed new development will be too close for them."

James and Sally were both alarmed over this news. "What can we do, this development has to be stopped." "Too right," replied Tony, "but how? There is no way we can use the fairies as an excuse to stop this building work going ahead. Who would believe us? If anyone did actually believe us then we would have the press all over the village. That in itself would chase the fairies away. We need the help of everyone in the village, we have to come up with a damn good reason just why we have to stop this development from happening."

"What can we do?" James and Sally both spoke at the same time. "We all need to put our heads together and come up with a plan between us. Maybe we need to discover a wild orchid growing on the site. A rare plant or animal has been known to stop developers in other areas. We really need to organise a village meeting, maybe someone will come up with an idea. We will have to act quickly."

"Could we call a village meeting maybe one week from today? We can quickly spread the news of the meeting by word of mouth." Sally was keen to help. "Seems like a good idea," replied Tony. "We can`t afford to wait much longer.

It would have been easiest to hold the meeting here, in the Duck and Cow, however it is possible someone from outside the village would be here in the pub, we don't want to be overheard."

We would be happy to host the meeting," said James looking at Sally for confirmation. "That would be great of you," thanked Tony. "I am working here for a few hours tomorrow evening, I should be able to let a few people know. We will have to be a bit careful, we want to have as many there as possible, but we don't want the whole village turning up, it could get a bit out of hand."

A week later several of the villagers did turn up at James and Sally's house for the meeting. Sharon and Dave from the Duck and Cow were the first to arrive. They had left Ben in charge of the pub. "If this is going to be a regular meeting, we will have to share the venue. It could be a bit of a squeeze, but we could have the next meeting in our living room at the back of the pub." "We can make this decision at the end of the meeting, we will have an idea by then of how often we will need to meet up, or if we do need to meet again at all. Hopefully we won't have to have too many meetings, let's hope someone can come up with an idea before too long. We really don't mind hosting," replied James. "We have though been wondering how many people will attend." Not surprisingly Tony was the next to arrive, only a minute or two after Dave and Sharon.

James had brought as many spare chairs that he could find, including a couple of folding chairs from the garden, and crammed them into the fortunately large living room. Sally always enjoyed playing host and had baked a few dozen biscuits for the event. She had organised a tray of mugs ready for tea and coffee, Sharon gave a hand with the refreshments.

Tony informed them he had spread the word around, about the meeting, but had been a bit selective. "If there are too many people here, it makes it difficult to make any plans, everyone ends up talking at the same time." In the end there were about a dozen people who came to the meeting.

At the meeting everyone looked to Tony to be the spokesperson. They raised a few ideas between them. Some of these suggestions were sensible, other were rather ludicrous. Dave seemed to vaguely remember he had once heard that the proposed development site was to be situated on some marshland and wondered if this could be a deterrent. "I will write to the council."

No one knew of any wild orchids or rare animals that could be living in the area where the proposed development site was, apart of course from the fairies. James asked about any historical sites, whether any battles had ever been fought in the area. No one knew, so James offered to look it up before they all got together again. Tony did look a bit doubtful, but guessed anything was worth a try.

Sharon said she would look up the proposed site to ensure it wasn't green belt land. They all presumed that this would have already been investigated though before the development was considered, but anything was worth trying.

Tony himself seemed a bit stumped, as if he had no idea what they could do to put a stop to the build. James and Sally had no idea if Tony really didn't know what to do about the development, or if he was considering something more out of the ordinary. They wondered if he just wanted to consider more down to earth ideas first. After about an hour or so the meeting about the development came to an end, most of the group stayed around for another warm drink and a general chit chat. They all knew a week probably wasn't long enough before the next meeting to investigate some of their suggestions, but they did not have the luxury of time on their side.

A week later, as agreed, they did meet up again at Dave and Sharon's, where they crammed into the living room at the back of the pub. None of the group were unduly surprised to find that no one had come across any solid ideas that would put a stop to the proposed new build. The new development was close to green belt land but not actually on it. Sally had spent some time trawling the internet looking up any rare flora or fauna that may have ever been seen in the area, but she could not find anything.

The nearest battle that had been fought in the area, was about fifteen miles away. Any marshland in the area was to be found was on the other side of the river, away from the development. Everything seemed to be stacked against them. "There doesn't seem to be anything we can do, the build will have to go ahead. It will drive the fairies away, and of course spoil the peacefulness of our village."

Once again they all looked to Tony, all of those present were hoping he could come up with some sudden, amazing reason as to why the development could not go ahead, but he looked as downcast as the rest of them. The meeting finished on a low note, everyone of them contemplating the effect of this new build on their own village life. Several agreed to write letters to the council to object, but with no definite, strong enough reason to stop the build, then they did wonder if all these letters would turn out be a bit futile.

No one was at all surprised, though all were very dismayed, when only a month or so after they had all met, the planning application was granted. It did not seem very long after this that heavy machinery and materials were moved on to the sight in order for the building work to start. When James and Sally called into the Duck and Cow, the talk invariably turned to the development, there was obviously a big resentment to it throughout the village.

James and Sally had to pass by the new development most days on their way to and from work. Soon after work started, a wooden hut appeared. This they found out was to house the security man who would be on site each evening and overnight, once the builders had left for the day.

James and Sally went for a stroll one evening a few days after the hut appeared. Their walk took them past the new development. By chance they got talking to the security man. This one was new, he had been brought in to replace the first security man, who they found out, had only lasted two days.

"He said he had seen a few strange sightings, he called them ghosts. He was convinced he had seen quite a few men, they were marching and were dressed in what looked like Roman clothes. Not only that, but he could only see them from their knees up, they didn't appear to have any lower legs. Have you heard owt like this tale before? We reckon he had had a few too many to drink. Not that he should have been drinking, not before coming to work. Have you ever seen owt like this?"

James and Sally had to confirm no, they had never seen anything like this, or heard of any sightings of ghosts like this in the area before. They did though give each other a knowing look, the kind of look that meant neither of them was at all surprised by this.

The security man was very talkative, he was obviously appreciating a bit of company. "I have been doing this job for a few years now, and spent many a night with only my own company. I have seen some strange sights during this time, but I don't believe in ghosts."

"Let's hope it stays quiet for you," said James. "I am sure there must be some logical explanation for what the other security man saw." With that James and Sally said goodbye and carried on with their walk.

They weren't home long before James gave Tony a call. He wanted to know Tony's opinion on this sighting. James was a bit curious to know if there really were any ghosts in the area, and why not, since there were already angels and fairies, not to mention a bit of time travel. Tony though was a bit vague with his answer and he didn't give a real explanation either way. "Ghosts of Roman soldiers, I have never heard of this before, but who knows." So James and Sally were none the wiser.

Not long after this Sally found herself near to the new development. School had now broken up for the Easter holiday and she had a bit more free time. While she was passing the development Sally paused for a short while to watch the builders. It filled her with dismay seeing the land being torn up, it was heart breaking knowing there was nothing she could do about it.

Today the weather had been good, especially warm and sunny, over the last few days though they had had a fair amount of rain. Sally had watched the weather forecast earlier, she had heard this good weather was here to stay for a few days at least. Sally now noticed though there were a few dark clouds looming. The clouds seemed to appear from nowhere. Sally only hoped that if it was going to rain she would get home in time, she was certainly not dressed for wet weather.

Sally was about to head for home, in case it did come on to rain. Just as she was setting off back she heard a shout. An accident had happened on the building site. The site was muddy, very slippery under foot. One of the workers had lost his footing, and had fallen against a large pile of bricks. The man went down on the floor, with a few of the bricks falling on to his leg.

Without giving it any thought, Sally rushed over to help the builder. It did not cross her mind she could be putting herself at risk. Several other builders also came over to help. Immediately one of the workers phoned for an ambulance, the injury to the leg certainly did not look good.

Sally knew some basic first aid. No one objected when she took charge. She instructed the builders to remove any debris away from the injured man, and she also made sure he was not moved at all. Sally had seemed to have forgotten about the conditions on the building site, without giving it any thought, she knelt down in the mud to try to talk and give some comfort to the injured builder.

Sally stayed with the injured man until the paramedics arrived, she had no idea how long this took. She found out the man was also called James, though he was always known as Jim. He was married with two young children. Whilst Sally stayed with Jim, the weather conditions had deteriorated and it had started to rain. It was raining very heavily by the time the paramedics arrived. One of the other builders had produced an umbrella from somewhere on the building site and he was standing holding it over Jim and Sally, at least it kept off the worst of the rain.

During this time Sally had been kneeling down trying to give some reassurance to Jim, she had only really been thinking of him. It was when she stood up, after the paramedics had arrived, she noticed, very close to where the casualty was lying, there was a flagstone, a certain flagstone, one which could only be found in this village. This flagstone also had a star and crescent moon on it.

When the paramedics had arrived Sally stepped back to allow them take over. They were able to give Jim some pain relief and immobilised his obviously broken leg before they got him into the warmth and safety of the ambulance. Sally didn't have time to say goodbye to Jim, but she knew that sometime over the next few days she would pop back to the office on the building site to see how he was.

Later of course, when James came home, she told him the story. He was a bit concerned about Sally, that she had not done herself any harm by being out in the cold and wet, especially kneeling down in the mud. "I had a shower as soon as I got back, and then spent an hour or so curled up with a book and a cup of hot chocolate. I will be fine."

Once she had told James the tale, Sally went to phone Tony and repeated the story. Tony was naturally concerned about the injured man, though he did state this kind of accident could happen on any building site, particularly with these wet conditions. Tony was though taken aback when Sally told him about the flagstone. "Are you sure it was a flagstone with a crescent moon and star? I didn't know there were any over there. I must try to see the site manager."

The following day Tony did manage to track down the site manager. The weather in Marton cum Tiddleworth had not improved as it should have done. The previous evening there had been a very spectacular thunderstorm. The building site looked muddier than ever.

Tony tried to explain to the site manager as best as he could without giving anything away, about the flagstones, how they should not be moved. The site manager though clearly did not want to listen, he very quickly dismissed all Tony was saying. He certainly refused to stop the build or to have any regard whatsoever for these flagstones.

Tony had no choice, but to give up, he knew the site manager was not going to take any notice. It was obviously going to take more than this one accident for anyone to take any notice. Tony only hoped that there would not be a fatal accident. He had no idea at all how he could convince anyone, without giving anything away, about the connection between the bad weather and the unusual flagstones.

CHAPTER EIGHTEEN

A week or two went by. The bad weather in Marton cum Tiddleworth continued. Sally`s parents came to stay for a few days. They were both surprised at how bad the weather was. "Usually you seem to have better weather than we do, I can`t believe the difference, considering we do not live too many miles apart," Sally`s mum commented.

The bad weather put a bit of a dampener on their plans for long walks in the countryside and barbecues. Instead they had a shopping trip to the nearby city. Surprisingly here the weather was a few degrees warmer with some sun and no dark clouds. They were able to have a pleasant boat trip on the river. "Maybe we will be able to have that barbecue this evening." No such luck though. When they got back to Marton cum Tiddleworth the weather here was just the same as it had been when they had left, grey skies, cooler and certainly looking as if more rain wasn't far away.

On the last night of their stay, they all went to have a meal at the Duck and Cow. The pub was once again busy. Tony was there, helping out behind the bar. Sally`s parents had met him a few times before, and had got to know him well on the day James and Sally moved into their cottage. This evening though they were only able to say a quick hello, Tony was too busy to talk. They ordered their drinks and then went to find a seat.

By the time they had finished eating the pub was becoming more quiet. Tony was able to come over for a chat. The conversation, naturally, turned to the weather. Tony, James and Sally had to be a bit careful about what they said in front of Sally's parents, the three of them, of course, knew the real reason for the bad weather.

Talk also turned to the subject of the new build. Tony mentioned that there had been another accident on the site. Fortunately it turned out to be not as serious as the one Sally witnessed. Was this just a coincidence though, the two accidents, or did health and safety need tightening up on the site? Could it also possibly be that there was another influence causing these accidents? Only time would tell, but hopefully before any more accidents happened.

On the walk home from the Duck and Cow, it had for the time being, stopped raining, but there were dark clouds looming. For the time of year it was not particularly warm. The four of them had watched the news on television before they set out. According to the weather forecast it should have been a good early summers evening with no clouds. "It is such a shame it is so cloudy, the sky here on a clear night is certainly something to be seen."

The following day, a Monday, Sally's parents left for home. James was back at work. Sally wasn't working, it was near the start of her maternity leave and Sally would not be going back to work for some time. It should have been a good time to start maternity leave, if only the weather would improve.

On this Monday morning the weather had improved slightly, for now at least it was not raining, just dull and overcast. Once her mum and dad had gone Sally took the opportunity to strip the beds and to hang out the washing. Sally spent an hour or two doing housework, then she was at a loss. Sally sat down for a while to put her feet up, but she couldn't settle, she was too restless. Sally knew she should be resting more, but she had always been active.

Sally felt like going for a walk, but not necessarily in this weather. Sally then had the idea to do something she didn't usually do by herself. Sally decided to pay a visit to the old Marton cum Tiddleworth. It would be good to see Sadie and Christine, if they were around and not too busy. It wasn't like having friends in the present day, when you could phone first to see if it was convenient to visit.

Sally did not have the fear of time travel that she had previously. She headed over to the old outbuilding and in no time at all had crossed the border with no problem. Over here the sky was blue with hardly a cloud. Sally was able to shed the jacket she had been wearing. Everything over here looked more attractive, the grass and trees appeared to be greener, and there was an abundance of wild flowers. Sally enjoyed the walk. Sally could not help thinking about her washing, wishing she had been able to bring it over here to dry.

Sally called on Sadie first. Sadie was at home, she was not exactly stressed, but she was clearly very busy. Sadie was trying to tidy the house, with a toddler tugging at her apron and a baby staring to cry" Ah, the poor wee one, a spot of teething bother, because of it she just won't settle for long."

Sally picked up the baby who immediately stopped crying and gave Sally a gummy smile. Sally told Sadie she was also planning to visit Christine. "I could go look for her now and take the children, it will give you a break." "That would be great," replied Sadie, "Can you manage?" Sally smiled, "it will give me a little bit of practice for the future, we will be fine. If Christine is not around we can go and look at the ducks."

Sally carried the baby the relatively short distance to Christine's house. The other children stayed close by, even the toddler was good and did not wander off. The children had met Sally a few times before, but they were still a little in awe of her. Christine was in, she was not as busy as Sadie and was happy to have a break. They decided to go and sit on the green anyway so that the children could watch the ducks.

Christine found a bit of stale bread for the ducks. She supervised the children feeding the ducks, while Sally fussed over the baby. After the ducks had been fed, they all sat on the grass together, Christine and Sally chatted while the children played happily in the warm sunshine.

Sally told Christine about the new development. Christine was interested to hear the latest news. "I know it won't ever affect me, but I don't like to think that the village will change so much in the future, you always imagine it will always be like this, quiet and peaceful." Sally reassured her that it hadn't changed too much over the next hundred years. "If this development does go ahead though, then I can see that one day this village will become a town. Any suggestions you have to stop the development will be welcome. Now planning permission has been granted and the building has started, it will take something big to stop it."

"I will have a think," replied Christine, "but if anyone were to have any ideas then it would be Tony." They both knew though that Tony himself was stumped. "If anything is going to put a stop to the build at this stage it will probably have to be some kind of incident on the building site itself. I have no idea what though. It is almost like waiting and hoping for a catastrophe to happen. We all want the build to stop, but certainly not at the cost of anyone's life."

For a while though Sally tried to take her mind off the miserable weather they were experiencing in Marton cum Tiddleworth of 2006, and managed to enjoy this moment. It was so pleasant sitting there in the warm sunshine watching the children playing contentedly together. The baby had not needed much persuading that she was tired, and she was now fast asleep in Sally's arms. Christine wanted to take the baby, she was concerned Sally might be getting a bit uncomfortable, Sally was not having that though. She reassured Christine she was just fine. Sally had realised how content she felt nursing this baby. The time could not come fast enough for her, and before too long, she knew she would be holding her own baby.

They sat there for the best part of an hour. Sally could have sat longer. She enjoyed chatting to Christine, she was sure the pair of them would never tire of swapping school stories, it was so interesting comparing the two centuries. Sally though felt it was now time to be taking the children back. As soft as the grass was, as pleasant the surroundings were, in her present condition there was only so long that Sally could sit comfortably on the ground. They gathered the children together. Christine returned to her own house and Sally took the children home.

"You have been gone awhile," said Sadie taking the baby from Sally. "Have all the children behaved themselves?" "They were no problem at all," replied Sally. Sadie had managed to tidy up a fair bit and was now peeling the potatoes for tea. "Will you be alright now if I return home?" asked Sally. "Certainly, you have helped a lot. It was good to have a bit of time to myself and collect my thoughts."

With that Sally said goodbye and made her way back home. What a difference a hundred years made. One side of the door was warm and sunny, on the other side it was raining yet again. Sally only had a thin jacket on, she had been plenty warm enough in 1906, but now with only the short walk across the garden Sally felt cold and damp. The

229

washing had been left hanging outside for the last few hours and was now almost as wet, it had barely dried at all.

Once inside Sally made herself a warm drink and made a start on their evening meal. It wouldn't be long before James was home.

Later that evening, together, they watched the evening news and the weather forecast. Sally had told James about her trip to the other side, as they tended to refer to Marton cum Tiddleworth of one hundred years ago. Sally talked about the good weather over there, how it had been a shame to return to this miserable weather. "I have been inside all day, but through the windows, the weather at work also looked good. It was only till I drove to less than a mile from home that the weather turned this miserable."

The weather forecast just then came on the television. Sally and James were both put out to hear the weatherman talk about the fine summer weather that was forecast for the entire country, and how it was set to continue for a few days yet. They both couldn't help wondering if the work force on the building site, particularly the manager could possibly conceive they were the cause of this unusual weather around here. Surely one of the main topics of conversation on the building site had to be this weather, it must surely be hampering progress.

CHAPTER NINETEEN

Over the next week or so the weather in Marton cum Tiddleworth didn't get any better. Sally had wanted to spend some of her free time at home pottering around the garden. The garden was very large and did need regular attention. Sally though, instead, was spending a lot of time away from home. She had several friends who lived not so far away and who were more than happy for her to visit. Sally was able to sit in their gardens and enjoy the good summer weather. Sally was reluctant to return the favours and invite friends back to Marton cum Tiddleworth because of the weather. She did vaguely mention the poor weather they were experiencing in Marton cum Tiddleworth, but none of her friends seemed to believe her.

During this time James took a week off work and they had a week away in Devon together. They were fortunate the good weather the rest of the country had been having continued. They had a lovely week away. As soon as they returned home, though, the weather was still all doom and gloom. The skies were grey as they drove back into Marton cum Tiddleworth and it was trying to rain. There were many large puddles around. As they drove past the building site it didn't look as if much more work had been done there, the whole building site did rather resemble a huge mud bath.

They met up with Tony that evening in the Duck and Cow. They had had a long drive back home from Devon and decided the evening meal in the pub would be a better idea than cooking. Tony had once again been to see the site manager. "I guess I knew it was a bit pointless, there has already been so much money spent on this site, it is probably too late to stop the building work now. I just felt that I had to do something. The whole village is beginning to wonder if the sun will ever shine here again. The site manger himself had grumbled somewhat over the bad weather. The work on the site has been delayed. The progress is much slower than had been planned. The builders were all finding the muddy conditions very hard to work in."

A few days after their return from Devon the weather did get dramatically worse. Sally was having an afternoon at home. She was catching up with the ironing from the holiday, she had not been able to dry any of the holiday washing outside, as she would have liked. Now yet again the weather was no better.

While she was ironing Sally put the television on to catch the news. Once again she saw the weather forecast, the majority of the country was enjoying a heat wave, not here though thought Sally. The sky outside appeared to be getting darker. It had been drizzling for most of the morning, the kind of fine drizzle that makes you wet through. Now though the rain was getting heavier. By the time Sally came to put the ironing away the rain was torrential. It was very dark outside, although it was still quite early, Sally had to put on the lights so she could see what she was doing.

Sally had just nicely put the lights on when they flickered. This was shortly followed by a big flash of lightening. After the lightening appeared Sally still instinctively counted, just as she used to do as a child. She did not get very far at all with the counting before there was a loud clap of thunder.

Sally had never been afraid of thunderstorms, but this one was close. Sally glanced out of the window. The rain was still torrential, she was glad she did not have to go out, however she was concerned about James driving home from work in it. It would be another hour or so before he would be home, the storm could well have passed over by then.

The rain though didn't stop, it continued as heavily as before. Their house on Whisper lane did not look out on to any roads, Sally could only wonder at the state of them. Sally though was mesmerised looking out on to the garden, there were big puddles on the lawn, and these were becoming larger with every minute that passed. Sally was beginning to think that before long their garden would be just one large pond.

Sally thought about their track, leading from the road, down to the house. This was mainly made up of gravel stones. Sally had never given it much thought before, but now she was worried that a lot of the gravel could have washed away, it may no longer be possible to drive down the track. Sally tried to phone James, but he was not answering. She left him a message on his phone. Sally had to presume the rain was once again only this bad around Marton cum

Tiddleworth, she wanted to warn James just how bad the weather was at home.

Sally could not get in touch with James, she had to wait anxiously for two hours. During the time Sally was waiting for James, the rain had barely let up. James, fortunately, was not that much later than usual. As expected there was very little rain around until he approached the outskirts of the village. James had eventually got Sally's message, but even so, he was still really taken aback as to how bad the weather actually was in Marton cum Tiddleworth.

Driving through the village James had to slow right down, the visibility was very poor. He could see why Sally had sent the warning. He stopped at the top of the track leading down to their cottage. It did look treacherous. James decided to leave his car parked as safely as possible at the top of the lane and then he walked the rest of the way home in the pouring rain. He was somewhat concerned about the surface of the lane and also about Sally's car, whether they would eventually be able to move it up the lane and onto higher, more firmer ground.

James got drenched walking down the lane, not usually a very long distance to his house, but today it felt much longer today. As soon as James got in he had to get straight in the shower before he and Sally were able to sit down to eat the evening meal. They had previously planned to pop up to the Duck and Cow before they ate, but this was now out of the question, this was now definitely an evening to stay in.

The following day was a Saturday, they hadn't been up for very long when Tony came to visit. James put the kettle on and made coffee, an automatic reaction these days when Tony called. The rain was still falling, but had now eased off a little. Tony had on a good pair of walking boots, he took these off in the porch, they really were muddy. Surprisingly though the rest of Tony, including his coat, was fairly dry.

Tony had called round to fill James and Sally in on the latest village news. The rain had been more devastating than anyone would have imagined. The river that ran close to the border of the village, had actually burst its banks and was now over flowing. At present it was only over flowing on to adjacent fields, and also on to the new development! Fortunately the flooding had not reached the village itself and so therefore none of the properties were affected.

Tony went on to explain how early the previous afternoon all the workmen had had to abandon all of the building work, even the security guard had not gone to work, there had been no point, even the most determined thief or vandal would not have been able to have gained access to the site.

James tried to put into words what the three of them were hoping for. "You don't think do you....?" "Yes," replied Tony, "you really never know, this torrential rain might now put a stop to the new development. Who would want to buy a house on this site knowing about this flood? It has never flooded here before. Now though it will take some time for the flood water to recede. Let's face it, the three of us here, and the rest of the villagers know it probably won`t stop raining until a decision has been made about the new development. I don't think we will have as much rain again as we had yesterday, but I really do think this rain will continue until a decision has been made."

"I have heard that a local TV reporter is going to come and have a look, the press are presumably wanting to do a story because of our unusual and very localised weather, particularly now the river has burst its bank." The three of them spent some time discussing the issue. None of them really wanted any news coverage for their village, but on the other hand, it could well turn out to be bad publicity for the new build.

When it was time for Tony to leave, James decided to walk part way with him to look at their track, to check it for any damage. The two of them walked up it together. Fortunately the track was not as bad as James had at first feared. He still however decided not to drive his car down the track until the weather had improved and it had dried off somewhat. The track was still quite muddy. James knew ideally this track could do with a better surface on it, but dreaded to think of the cost. He would have to ask Sally`s dad for a rough estimate.

The rain continued over the weekend, it was not as bad has it had been on Friday, but it was still persistent. James and Sally went out both Saturday and Sunday to escape the miserable weather. They didn't have to go too far out of the village before they found some sun.

There was a local television reporter in the village when they returned back home on Saturday. Marton cum Tiddleworth was featured on the local news. The building site did look very desolate, it was not a good advert if anyone had been thinking of buying one of the houses. James and Sally called in at the Duck and Cow on Sunday evening. The new build and also the storm were, unsurprisingly, the main topics of conversation.

The following morning there was an emergency meeting at the building site to discuss the damage the rain had caused, and also the likelihood that this area might ever have such problems with flooding again. Everyone at the meeting were scratching their heads over the bad weather that this village was experiencing.

"It is as if these villagers living here have managed to plan this deliberately in order to stop the development. Not one of them wanted these houses to be built here." "No one though can possibly have any influence on weather like this."

It was a hard decision, but a decision had to be made. Following careful consideration of many factors involved, the building company and the local town council had to agree to stop the building work. A lot of money had already been spent on this site and this would now be lost. They all knew though by now if they did continue with the development these houses would be hard to sell. Now that this land had been flooded once, there was a strong chance it could happen again. It was a huge decision, but everyone at the meeting reluctantly agreed the building work had to stop.

It did seem as soon as this decision was made the rain stopped. The sky was still grey, but the rain did actually stop falling. A week or two after building work had stopped and the flood water and mud had receded, a few of the villagers went to the site one Saturday morning. With some effort and a lot of team work they managed to restore the moon and star flagstones to their original position. James now found, as he was helping, like previously when he was moving the flagstones in his garden, that these flagstones were also replaced without too much effort.

It was an amazing sight to see, once the flagstones had been replaced, the grey skies lifted and the sun began to shine. A few weeks later the building site was cleared of all building materials and also the hut, that had been used as the site office, was taken down. The villagers were pleased to see such a good job was made of clearing the site, there was very little rubbish left behind. They all knew eventually the grass would grow back and this area would look just as it had done previously.

During the period of time, while the site was being cleared, Tony was walking past. He noticed some of the workmen were somewhat puzzled that the star and moon flagstones had been moved. Tony only spoke briefly to these workmen, only to comment on the good weather, he did not want to enlighten them on just how the flagstones had been moved.

CHAPTER TWENTY

Sally woke up early one morning during her maternity leave and gave a big stretch. Today she had no specific plans, just a bit of light housework. Sally stayed in bed for a few moments, listening to James getting ready for work. Sally only had about two weeks to go before the baby was due, she was so looking forward to holding her own baby, but also felt this last bit of time should be rather precious. After a little deliberation with herself, Sally decided today to make one more trip over to Marton cum Tiddleworth of one hundred years ago, while she still could do so. Sally had no idea how many more opportunities she would have to go over there once the baby had been born.

Sally had become good friends with both Sadie and Christine and was looking forward to seeing them again. Sally set off early afternoon. Her mum had already phoned, as she did so now on a daily basis. Sally felt relieved that she did not have to explain her outing to her mum, as her mum was always concerned about her these days. Sally had led her to presume that she would be sat at home with her feet up.

The weather was lovely, not too hot, but no sight of any rain, there had not been any rain in the village since the building work had stopped. As Sally walked the short distance through the old outbuilding across to the other side, to Sadie's house, she could feel a niggle or two. Sally was not unduly worried, she had done a lot of reading up on pregnancy and childbirth and knew about Braxton Hicks contractions, she knew they could happen for a week or so before birth and did not necessarily mean labour had started.

As she walked Sally caressed the bump. The bump had been active for the last week or so, causing some discomfort, today though the baby seemed to be quieter.

Sally soon got to Sadie's house. Sadie was busy as usual, but she was still pleased to see Sally. Sadie made them both a hot drink and insisted that Sally sit in a comfortable chair. They kept up a good conversation, though throughout all this time Sadie didn't sit, she was always on the go. Sally attempted a couple of times to get up and give Sadie a hand, but Sadie would not allow her. "Once that baby of yours has arrived you will never have a minute to yourself, make the most of any free time now."

Sally stayed for the best part of an hour, but then had to get up to go, she also wanted to go and visit Christine. However as Sally did stand up to leave she felt a strange sensation and a flood of water. Sally had a sudden realisation of what was happening, surely not here, not right now. Sally cursed herself for having come here today. She hadn't told anyone, not even James, about her plan for today, no one knew where she was. Sally now just wanted to be at home, in her own bed with James and her midwife there.

Sadie though was so competent and practical. She immediately knew of course, from her own experience, what was happening. Sadie sent her oldest child off to fetch Christine and also Ted. Sadie helped Sally upstairs, into her own bed and provided her with a clean nightdress.

Sally felt in a daze, she did not want to be here, but had no choice, she could not walk home now, the walk home, not usually much of a distance, was too far to even consider trying at present. Sally by now knew that she was in fact in established labour, those Braxton hicks contractions had turned out to be the real thing. The contractions had now become much more frequent and quite painful. Once Sally was tucked up in Sadie's bed she was able to think more logically and ask a few questions of Sadie.

The first one was of course her baby's safety. "If the baby is born here, will it be safe to take the baby home to 2006?" "Yes, of course. This baby is yours, it belongs to 2006 not this century, everything will be fine. Ted will send for Tony, you can ask him as well." Sally looked surprised, she had not considered Tony, the one person she really wanted right now was James, but he would be hard at work, she had no way of getting in touch with him from here. It would be sad if he were to miss the birth of his first child. If though Tony were able to come here he would know how to get in touch with James.

Sally could not think of this any longer as another now more painful contraction swept over her. Sadie was there at her side, she was a great comfort. The pain eased. Sally turned to a more practical question. "Just who will deliver this baby, it should have been delivered by my own midwife in hospital." Sally knew there was no way on earth they could get her own midwife.

"I hope you can trust me," replied Sadie, "your baby won`t be the first one I have delivered, I have delivered a few of the babies born in this village over the last few years."

Sally had not considered this, she did not even know this about Sadie. Sally though knew she could put her trust in Sadie, that both she and the baby would be in safe hands. Sally had no idea what she would tell her own midwife when they met up again about who had delivered the baby, or the place of birth. Somehow this small matter was not important right now.

In between contractions Sally could hear voices from downstairs. She could make out Christine`s voice. Sadie told her that Christine had come to help out with the children while she herself was otherwise occupied with delivering this baby. "I am so sorry," replied Sally, "I did not mean to put anyone out. I so should not have come here today." "Don't be silly, you would not have known this baby was going to be born today, I am so pleased and feel quite honoured that I am able to deliver your baby."

Labour progressed as expected. Sally did find the contractions to be very painful, but with Sadie's calm manner and relaxing words of encouragement Sally did find that she could cope with the pains. Sally had no idea about the passage of time. She seemed to have been here in this comfortable bed for ever but it must only have been two or three hours since she had left home. Sally even managed to drift off to sleep for a short while.

As Sally was woken with another contraction, she could make out talking from downstairs, and another very familiar voice, but surely not, she must be dreaming! Only a minute or two later Sally was amazed to see James walk into the room, she suddenly felt she could cope with anything. James walked over and gave Sally a huge hug, he certainly looked very relieved to see her.

"How on earth did you know I was here? I am so sorry I did not let you know I was coming over here today." "Don't worry," replied James, "you seem to be in good hands. Ted managed to send a message to Tony, Marton cum Tiddleworth style, to let him know what was happening. Tony phoned me at work, I came as quickly as I could. I would not want to miss this for anything."

Sally wanted to sink back into the comfy pillows and let everyone else take control. There was no chance for this to happen though as another very painful contraction took over. The contractions now seemed to be more frequent and more painful. Sally didn't know if she could take much more. She was so grateful to have James and Sadie at her side, but she also could not help think about the pain relief she would have been able to have in a modern day hospital. Still no point on dwelling on this right now.

Once this contraction had passed over Sally asked if it were possible for Tony to pop in. At this suggestion, once again Sadie looked a bit disapproving, it was bad enough having one man in the delivery room. Still though Sadie was all too aware what Sally wanted to ask of Tony and knew she would remain rather anxious until she had spoken to Tony. Sadie therefore called him up. Tony was able to put both Sally and also James at ease over their concern about time travel and the baby. "It is right that people from 1906 cannot travel to 2006, but this baby will be fine. This baby belongs to 2006 rather than this period of time, the baby was conceived there. Like all of the children of 2006, from the village of Marton cum Tiddleworth, this child will be happy and healthy in both worlds."

Tony only stayed for a few minutes, then he left Sally to get on with the progress of childbirth. Sadie found it to be a bit strange having James there present throughout the labour, she had heard this was normal for 2006 and felt she could somehow manage to accommodate James being there. He didn't seem to be making a fuss at all and was actually being quite helpful. He did seem to have a calming effect over Sally, he certainly showed Sally a lot of sympathy and gave her comfort to enable her to cope with the labour pains.

Sally felt more at ease with having James there. It did occur to Sally she should suggest they should go home, back to 2006 and her own bed. As soon, though, as Sally thought about going home to her own bed, she started to feel the vague urge to push. Sally now knew there was no way now she could go back home, this baby was determined to be born here in 1906.

Sadie had, obviously, been spending a lot of her time throughout the labour, with Sally. Sally was amazed at her ability to also run the household, to ensure all the farming jobs were getting done, that the children were behaving and to have all this time to spend with herself making sure she was comfortable. Sadie remained so calm and efficient. Sally still felt somewhat guilty about using Sadie and Ted's bed, but Sadie put her completely at ease.

Sadie had popped out of the room for a moment or two. James had been watching Sally constantly, he sensed that something was happening. "I think this baby is going to be here very soon, please can you go and get Sadie." It was as if Sadie had stationed herself right outside the bedroom, she was there straight away as soon as James had opened the door. Sadie was also well prepared with a bowl of hot water and soap.

Sadie gave James another warning about his behaviour in the delivery room, that he had to sit still and not interfere. Sadie had never before delivered a baby while the father had been present, she was worried he might get in the way, or worse be sick or even pass out.

Sally was made as comfortable as possible. Sadie fussed about, getting towels ready and also a blanket for the baby. Within a short space of time, with no fuss or palaver Sally and James first baby was born. With no previous experience of childbirth, Sally could not help think this was how childbirth should be. The bed was so comfy, the atmosphere very calm and relaxed and Sadie really was very efficient.

James did prove to be very useful in what was now the delivery room. He had a calming influence on Sally and was able to pass anything to Sadie that she needed. Sadie was certainly impressed. James even had the initial awesome moment of holding his new baby daughter while again the afterbirth was efficiently delivered and tidied away by Sadie. The baby was beautiful, she had of course cried initially straight after she was born, now though she lay contentedly in James arms.

Sadie was so efficient, in no time at all Sally was feeling refreshed and clean and was once more comfortable in bed. With Sally's permission both Christine and Tony popped in. Christine didn't stay long, only long enough to have a quick cuddle with the new baby, and long enough to reassure herself that both new mother and baby were well.

Tony stayed for longer. James and Sally were both so relieved that the birth had gone well, and now they had their beautiful little daughter. They both now had to think practically. They both knew once again they were beholden to Tony to come up with a solution for getting both Sally and the baby safely back to home to 2006.

There was no way Sally could manage the walk home, there was certainly no handy wheelchair so James could push Sally and the baby home. They both also knew once they arrived home they would have a bit of explaining to do, as to why they hadn't contacted their own midwife at the start of labour! They couldn't exactly have expected her to pop over to this time period to deliver the baby!

"If you would trust me to fly you both home then I promise I will keep you both safe," Tony addressed Sally. "Will you though be able to hold on tightly to this precious little bundle while we are flying?"

Sally looked astonished. This method of transport home had not occurred to her. Faced though with any other possibilities, it did seem to be the best solution. Sally knew she had to put her trust in Tony and go along with this plan. Tony turned to Sadie and James, "we need to keep everything as simple as possible for when we return to 2006. You will have to tell a small white lie to the midwife. Please just tell her the baby came quickly and was born at home before either of you could let anyone know. The midwife though will need to see the placenta. Please James can you take it back with you?"

James was a bit bemused, but he knew he had to do it. He was once again very impressed that Tony managed to take control and plan all these details. James, like Sally, was so overwhelmed with the day he was so grateful to Tony for taking charge.

Sadie assisted Sally in getting out of bed and down the stairs. Sally had been using Sadie's nightclothes during the labour and delivery. Now though Sally was back in her own clothes that she had put on at the start of the day, the baby was wrapped up well in an old blanket. James left for home first, so he was able to arrive there before Sally. Ted had managed to take a short break from work so he could a quick peek at the baby. Ted then walked so far back with James. James knew Sally would be safe with Tony, but he could still not help feeling rather anxious.

Five or ten minutes after James had set off it was then Sally's turn to head off home. Sally, previously, had so wanted to do this, fly with an angel, but today of all days! Tony unfurled his wings, Sally was surprised at how broad his back was. With help from Sadie and Tony, Sally, somewhat ungainly, climbed on to Tony's back. Christine handed over the baby and with barely a jolt Tony took off.

Sally concentrated on making sure she didn't fall off, she was surprised though at how comfortable it was, more like sitting in a soft chair, rather than a piggy back ride on a friends back. Sally held her new baby daughter tightly to her, she was still able to look down as they flew over the fields and trees, not too far below. As they flew Sally glanced down at her daughter, she was sleeping peacefully, blissfully unaware of all the fuss that her birth had caused.

Very soon after they had become airborne, Tony, Sally and the baby landed very close to the house on Whisper lane. The journey had been very short. James was there waiting for them, he was relieved when they landed safely. Tony only stayed around long enough to see that Sally and baby were safely inside. Once inside Sally went with the baby to the bedroom. She dressed the new born baby in a nappy and baby clothes she had previously got ready to take into hospital. Sally and James rested on the bed, cuddling their new daughter.

Once they were settled and comfortable Sally phoned the midwife and explained to her how the baby had arrived sooner and quicker than they had expected, that there had been no time to alert anyone labour had started. Sally continued with the tale, how James had had to deliver the baby, but reassured the midwife they were both safe and well. The midwife did seem a bit surprised since first babies did not usually come this quickly, she informed Sally she would call and see her as soon as she could.

Sally had met her own midwife several times previously during ante natal check-ups. Fortunately it was the same midwife who was working today. Within half an hour of the telephone call the midwife was there. She did seem a bit surprised to see both Sally and the baby looking so well, and somehow it didn't look as if the baby had only been born less than an hour before. The midwife completed the mother and baby and removed the placenta, which was still in the same old milk pail.

Sally had of course arranged to have her baby in the hospital. The midwife was able to agree with Sally that there was now no point in them going into hospital, Sally was able to stay at home in her own surroundings and comfortable bed.

Once the midwife had left, with a promise that she would be back the following day, Sally sank back into the pillows and gave the baby her first feed. She felt so content and remarkably relaxed, probably more so than if she had given birth in hospital. Sally could hear James pottering around downstairs, putting some kind of meal together.

Sally knew that once she had finished feeding the baby she would have to phone her mum with the news. Sally would leave it up to James to phone his parents. The midwife had not questioned her about the fact that the baby did appear to be a few hours old when she had visited. However Sally knew her mum might be a bit put out to find out that her first grandchild had been born a few hours ago and she was only just getting to find out, Sally knew she would just have to be a bit vague about the exact time of birth.

Sally didn't have to worry too much since her mum was so thrilled with the news. Her mum of course wanted to know all the details, she was also surprised over the rather quick delivery and that the baby had been born at home. "As long as you are both well, this is more important. Does my granddaughter have a name yet?" Sally and James had spent some time previously in discussing the name, Sally was now happy to share this with her mum. "Sophie Antonia." "What a lovely name for my first grandchild, Antonia is rather an unusual choice."

Sally and her mum decided on the phone that, as they had previously planned, both her parents would visit the following day and then her mum would stay on to help for a few days. Once she had put the phone down Sally sank back into the pillows. She knew her life wouldn't be the same again, but she felt so well blessed.

EPILOGUE

Following the arrival of Sophie Antonia life returned to normal, that is as much as it could do with a new baby around. Sally was soon up and about after the birth and took to motherhood very easily. Sally just felt it a shame that before too long she would have to return to work.

A few weeks after the delivery the weather was again lovely and warm, in fact the weather had been good ever since the new development had come to an end. Sally had got on with some of the housework in the morning, she then fed and changed Sophie and brought her out into the garden. Sally sat for a while with Sophie and ate a peaceful lunch. After lunch Sally got up and walked just a few yards away from Sophie to check on the washing. When she glanced back at Sophie Sally just stopped in her tracks. Her first concern was for the safety of her baby, but then Sally realised that Sophie was quite safe. She found herself looking at a most beautiful sight. Hovering around the edge of the Moses basket, where Sophie lay peacefully sleeping, there were about twenty to thirty fairies. The fairies appeared to be sprinkling Sophie with fairy dust. Sally felt that this was just pure magic, she just wished that James could have been there to have also witnessed this amazing sight. This surely must be Marton cum Tiddleworth`s own unique way of welcoming the new baby Sophie into the village.

Lightning Source UK Ltd.
Milton Keynes UK
UKOW02f2005140916

283004UK00001B/6/P